# More Tales from the Crystal Caves
## Friends Forever

promise to do my best. I promise to
work hard to care for the world and
its plants, animals and children.
This is the Fairy Bear Promise."

**Julie Sykes** lives with her family, their wolf and a flying carpet in a cottage in Hampshire. Julie first wrote about Fairy Bears after meeting Glitter the Fairy Bear in her back garden. When Julie isn't busy writing, she spends her time eating cake and having flying races with her Fairy Bear friends.

Read more sparkly stories in
*Tales from the Crystal Caves*

Visit the secret world of the Fairy Bears and explore the magical Crystal Caves . . .

www.fairybearsworld.com

# More Tales from the Crystal Caves
## Friends Forever

## Julie Sykes

Illustrated by Samantha Chaffey

MACMILLAN CHILDREN'S BOOKS

*Fairy Bears: Blossom* first published 2010 by Macmillan Children's Books
*Fairy Bears: Sparkle* first published 2010 by Macmillan Children's Books
*Fairy Bears: Primrose* first published 2010 by Macmillan Children's Books

This bind-up edition published 2012 by Macmillan Children's Books
a division of Macmillan Publishers Limited
20 New Wharf Road, London N1 9RR
Basingstoke and Oxford
Associated companies throughout the world
www.panmacmillan.com

ISBN 978-1-4472-1373-4

1 3 5 7 9 8 6 4 2

A CIP catalogue record for this book is available from
the British Library.

Printed and bound by CPI Group (UK) Ltd, Croydon CR0 4YY

# Contents

Firefly Meadow

Sycamore

GRAND DOOR

Caves for Fairy Bears who work for King & Queen

Turquoise Chamber

Diamond Arch

MAIN TUNNEL

To The Royal Caves

ROYAL TUNNEL

Whispering Pool

Rocky Island

Rowing Lake

Honey Bridge

Tree     Firefly Meadow

Nectar Cave

DiamondDell

Starlight Cave

Crystal Maze

Ruby Grotto

Hospital Cave

School Caves

Air Ball Stadium

To The Home Caves

Play Park

To Royal Theatre

Underground Stream

*For Alistair, William,*
*and for Sarah, my big little sis*

# Prologue

At the bottom of Firefly Meadow, not far from the stream, stands a tall sycamore tree. The tree is old with a thick grey trunk and spreading branches. Hidden amongst the branches is a forgotten squirrel hole. If you could fly through the squirrel hole and down the inside of the tree's hollow trunk, you would find a secret door that leads to a special place. Open the door and step inside the magical Crystal Caves, home of the Fairy Bears.

The Fairy Bears are always busy. They work hard caring for nature and children everywhere. You'll have to be quick to see them, and you'll have to believe in magic.

Do you believe in Fairy Bear magic?
Can you keep a secret? Then come on
in – the Fairy Bears would love to meet
you.

# Blossom the Brave

# Chapter One

The noise coming from the class cave was deafening as timid Blossom went inside and looked around anxiously for someone she knew. Her friend Sparkle hadn't arrived yet and Dizzy and Sunny were chattering with a large group of Fairy Bears. Blossom hesitated, feeling too shy to join the group. Across the cave the magic mirror seemed to wink at her. Blossom stared at it and the mirror winked again. Was it calling her over? Shyly, Blossom went and looked into the rectangular glass surrounded by tiny crystals, and blushed as her own face stared back at her. She was a small Fairy Bear with pretty pale-gold fur, pink wings, big brown eyes and a button black nose. Her reflection blushed too, then quickly faded to be replaced by a slim girl with curly brown hair pulled into an untidy ponytail. The girl was acting on a stage but she didn't seem to be enjoying herself. Her face was tense and she held her body stiffly.

"Poor thing," whispered Blossom, feeling her own stomach flutter nervously in sympathy.

The picture faded in a swirl of pink mist

and was replaced with an image of Coral. Blossom spun round, wondering if Coral had seen the nervous-looking girl too, but to her surprise she was alone. Coral was on the other side of the class combing her pure-white fur with a bored expression on her face.

Miss Alaska came into the room and the Fairy Bears scurried to their seats. Sparkle had arrived and Blossom sat down gratefully next to her friend.

"Good morning, class," said Miss Alaska, smiling. "Today I have chosen another Fairy Bear to go out on a task."

The Fairy Bears rustled their wings in excitement. The tasks were very important. You had to pass them all to be allowed to move up to the senior class. Miss Alaska was working her way through the junior class, choosing one Fairy Bear at a time to perform their first task.

It's going to be Coral, thought Blossom, remembering the pictures in the magic mirror. Coral loved acting so she would probably be asked to help the girl with the curly hair.

"Before I tell you who I've picked, let's say the Fairy Bear Promise. Blossom, are you with us or are you enjoying a lovely daydream?"

The class laughed and Blossom blushed, her pale-gold cheeks suddenly matching the pink of her wings. She laid her wand on her stone desk and, folding her wings behind her, held Sparkle and Sunny's paws. With tightly closed eyes Blossom began to chant.

"I promise to do my best. I promise to work hard to care for the world and all its plants, animals and children. This is the Fairy Bear Promise."

When she opened her eyes Miss Alaska
was holding up a sycamore leaf. The class
cave was so silent Blossom
could hear the moon clock
whirring softly on the
cave wall.

"Congratulations,
Blossom! Today you

are going out on your first task!" said Miss Alaska dramatically.

"Hooray!" cheered Sparkle and Sunny loudly.

"*Me?*" squeaked Blossom in alarm.

"Yes, you," replied Miss Alaska kindly. She handed Blossom the sycamore leaf. "Your task is written here."

Blossom quickly read the task and then reread it to check she'd got the details right.

"It's a good-luck task," she shyly announced. "I must sprinkle a girl called Chloe with good-luck stars. She's acting the part of Alice in a play called *Alice in Wonderland*. It's the lead role. Chloe wasn't meant to be the star. She was the understudy, but the girl who was playing Alice broke her ankle in a roller-skating accident."

"Why did Blossom get that task?" called

out Coral. "She doesn't know anything about acting. I'm the best actress in the school."

Blossom's wings quivered. Perhaps there had been a mistake? But Miss Alaska didn't think so.

"This task is for Blossom," she said firmly. "Don't forget to test your wand before you start. Good luck, Blossom."

Hesitantly Blossom picked up her wand. It was silver with a pink diamond set in the star at the wand's tip. The wand was new, a present from her mum and dad for her birthday last month, and Blossom was still getting used to it.

"Go on," said Sparkle encouragingly.

Tightly gripping the wand, Blossom waved it in the air. There was a loud squeak and then a stream of pink stars floated out from the tip. The stars seemed to

dance in the air as they formed a picture.

"A mouse!" exclaimed Blossom.

The pink star mouse flicked its tail and then evaporated. The class roared with laughter and clapped. Blossom blushed with pleasure as she walked to the cave door.

"Squeak, squeak!" said Coral spitefully as Blossom passed her. "Blossom the timid mouse. You won't pass this task. Even your wand knows you're not brave enough to complete it."

"Yes I am," protested Blossom. But Blossom's insides were trembling like butterfly wings in a storm. Did she really have the courage to solve her first task?

# Chapter Two

Clutching her wand in one paw and the sycamore leaf in the other, Blossom flew out of the school caves towards the Main Tunnel. It was busy with grown-up Fairy Bears going out for the day and Blossom hovered for ages in the side tunnel waiting for a gap big enough for her to fly out and join them, too shy to push in. Her journey ended at the foot of the gnarled root staircase that led to the Grand Door, the main way in and out of the sycamore tree that hid the Crystal Caves. Blossom waited patiently at the back of the queue for her turn to climb the staircase, but each time she got closer to the stairs she was squeezed back again by the jostling crowd. At last she gave up, deciding to wait for the crowd to disappear.

"Hello, are you all right?"

At first Blossom didn't realize the friendly-looking Fairy Bear with chocolate-coloured fur and green wings was talking to her.

"I'm Racer," he said. "You're in Miss Alaska's class, aren't you? Are you going out on your first task?"

Blossom nodded. She'd seen Racer around the school. He was a popular Fairy Bear in the seniors and often went out on tasks. Managing to find her voice she said quietly, "I'm Blossom."

"You'll never get your turn hanging back

like that," said Racer. "You have to be more confident. Stick with me and I'll show you what to do."

Blossom joined Racer at the back of the

queue. Each time someone knocked into him he didn't wobble or step back. Blossom copied him, keeping close to his side, and soon it was their turn to climb the staircase. Racer bounced up the stairs two at a time and vanished through the enormous Grand Door. Blossom followed, but then stopped inside the tree trunk, blinking rapidly as her eyes adjusted to the dark.

"Boo!" said Racer, chuckling as Blossom jumped. "I thought I'd wait for you, seeing as it's your first time. You look nervous."

"I am," Blossom admitted.

"Well, don't be," said Racer, encouragingly. "Once you get started, you'll be fine. The tasks are great fun."

"Thanks!" Blossom felt more confident as she flew up the inside of the tree with Racer. There were Fairy Bears all around her, their wings humming musically as they flew towards the pale circle of light shining through the squirrel hole near the top of the tree.

It was a beautiful day outside. The stream sparkled in the sunlight and Firefly Meadow was bursting with colourful flowers. Racer somersaulted in delight.

"Good luck, Blossom! You can't fail on a day like this."

Dipping his green wings in a goodbye salute, he sped off across the meadow. Watching him go, Blossom suddenly felt less confident. Why had Miss Alaska picked her for this task? Blossom was hopeless at acting. And she didn't feel ready to go out on her own. Should she turn back and ask Miss Alaska to give the task to someone else?

"I can't do that!" said Blossom suddenly. Giving up before she'd even tried would mean failing her first task and staying in Miss Alaska's class for another year. It would also mean failing Chloe. Remembering Chloe's worried face gave Blossom courage.

Blossom hovered in the air while she studied the map on the sycamore leaf. She carefully remembered the directions before wrapping the leaf tightly round her wand. Chloe was acting in a small theatre on the edge of a town. It was a long way from the Crystal Caves.

"Chloe, here I come," said Blossom, flying across the stream at the bottom of the meadow.

Blossom usually loved flying, but today she was too nervous to enjoy it. The closer she came to the theatre, the more uncomfortable she felt. Her tummy was fizzing like a fireworks display and her wings tingled. It was exhausting! Flying over a park, a few streets away from the theatre, Blossom was tempted to soar down for a rest. The park was green and inviting, with lots of bushes and trees. Blossom hesitated but then continued on her way, scared that if she stopped she might not have the courage to go on with her journey.

Minutes later she arrived. The theatre's huge glass windows and doors were all tightly shut. Blossom hovered outside, wondering how to get in. Opening doors by magic took a lot of energy, and Blossom wasn't strong enough to do it yet. Maybe there was a back entrance? Blossom flew

over the building to the car park behind.
A man was vigorously sweeping the
pavement. Behind him, the theatre's back
door was propped open with a chair.
Unseen, Blossom dived through the door
and into a long corridor that had more
doors on either side.

"Dressing rooms," said Blossom.

Miss Alaska had taken them on a tour
of the Royal Theatre in the Crystal Caves
and they'd seen dressing rooms there. Some
of the doors were open and Blossom flew
in and out of the rooms until she reached
the last door. It was ajar and Blossom
could hear a girl talking inside. Was it
Chloe? Quietly she flew into the room,
keeping close to the ceiling so she wouldn't
be noticed. Blossom recognized Chloe
immediately from her picture in the magic
mirror. She was standing in the middle

of the room, wearing a blue dress with a sparkling white apron, rehearsing her lines.

"Curiouser and curiouser," said Chloe, holding out her arms. "I seem to be stretching. Goodbye feet . . ."

Chloe acted out her body growing taller, cricking her neck sidewise as her head hit an imaginary ceiling. Blossom was transfixed. Not wanting to miss a second of Chloe's amazing acting, she fluttered closer and landed on the dressing-table mirror.

"What's that?" said Chloe, stepping forward. "Oh!" she gasped, covering her mouth with her hands in surprise.

Suddenly Blossom realized that Chloe had stopped acting and was looking straight at her.

"Am I dreaming?" Chloe asked hesitantly. "What are you?"

Blossom's wings went ice cold as Chloe's

face came nearer. If Blossom was braver, she could have reached out and touched Chloe on the nose with her wand.

"I thought you were a bee but you're not, are you? You look like . . ." Chloe hesitated. "You look like a little bear with wings."

"Hello," squeaked Blossom, struggling to find her voice. "I'm a Fairy Bear. My name's Blossom."

# Chapter Three

Blossom explained about Fairy Bears as Chloe listened, enthralled.

"And we help animals, plants and children who need us," she finished up, twirling her wand.

Chloe looked like she might burst with excitement. "Why are you here? Are you going to help someone?"

Blossom was about to answer her when she heard a funny shuffling noise in the corridor outside. Chloe's face fell. Guiltily she turned to face the door as a girl with shiny long blonde hair hopped into the room. The girl's right foot was in a pink plaster cast and she was walking with the help of crutches. Blossom fled back up to the ceiling.

"Hurry up," said the girl to Chloe. "You're needed onstage."

Blossom was surprised by the girl's unfriendly tone, but she was even more surprised by Chloe's reaction. Chloe's confident manner drained away.

"S-s-s-sorry, Katie," she stuttered. "I was practising my lines."

"Let's hope you get them right," said Katie sweetly. She tapped the floor with her crutch. "You didn't yesterday."

"It was only my second time," Chloe protested.

Katie ignored her.

"I can't believe I broke my ankle,"

she muttered as she left the room. "I was brilliant as Alice. The show's going to be ruined now."

Thinking that Chloe might be about to cry, Blossom fluttered down and landed in the palm of her hand. Chloe brightened and

Blossom was glad she'd acted impulsively. If she'd stopped to think about what she was doing, she'd probably have been too shy to get so close.

"I have to go," Chloe sighed. "It's the dress rehearsal."

Blossom twiddled her wand. This was her chance. She would tell Chloe that she was here to help *her* and sprinkle her with magic good-luck stars. She flew into the air, her wand poised ready to cast her spell, but Chloe was in too much of a hurry to notice. With a quick wave, she rushed from the room.

"Wait!" cried Blossom.

She flew after Chloe but another door opened in the corridor and two children squeezed out of it. They were dressed identically, with massive fake tummies that wobbled when they walked.

"Hi, Chloe," they called as they wobbled towards her.

Blossom followed the trio up one flight of stairs and along another corridor until they were backstage. A large group of children was crowded round a hassled-looking lady clutching a clipboard.

"Alice," she said, ticking her off on a list. "Tweedledum and Tweedledee. Fantastic! Now you're all here we can start. Alice, you're on first."

Someone handed Chloe a book as she nervously went and sat in the middle of the stage. The lady with the clipboard watched from the front. Katie was there, sitting in the second row, her crutches propped up against the seats.

"When you're ready," the lady called.

Blossom flew to the stage and hovered by the curtains. She guessed that the clipboard

27

lady was the director of the show. Poor Chloe looked so frightened. Her green eyes were enormous and when she opened her mouth to say her first line all that came out was a croak.

"Come on, Chloe," Blossom whispered encouragingly.

Clearing her throat, Chloe tried again.

"I'm bored," she sighed, flicking through the book. "There aren't any pictures to look at."

Chloe's acting was nothing like it had been in her dressing room. Her body was stiff and her voice wobbly. Plenty of the cast forgot their lines and there was lots of giggling as the director bellowed prompts from the front. But when

Chloe forgot her lines she took it very seriously, blushing furiously, her eyes sliding to Katie who responded with a scowl. Chloe's confidence had ebbed away and the more nervous she became the more lines she got wrong. At the end of the last scene the director sighed heavily as she stood up.

"That was not your best acting," she announced to everyone. "I can only hope that you are saving yourselves for the first performance tomorrow. Chloe, you need to go home and learn your lines."

Tears welled in Chloe's eyes. She hung her head so no one could see her as she rushed back to her dressing room. Blossom raced after her, only just making it into the room before Chloe shut the door.

"I thought you did really well," she said, hovering in front of her.

"Oh! You're still here," said Chloe,

brushing her tears away and managing a small smile. "I was awful. I know my lines off by heart but when I'm onstage I can't remember them. It doesn't matter how hard I practise. I'll never be as good as Katie. She was brilliant. Everyone said so."

"You have to stop comparing yourself to Katie," said Blossom sensibly.

"It's not that easy. Tracy, the lady in charge, is her mum so Katie comes to the theatre every time we rehearse. It's bad enough knowing she's watching without all the mean comments she makes."

"She must be really disappointed to miss out on playing the leading role," said Blossom sympathetically.

"She is," said Chloe, wriggling out of her costume. "But she shouldn't take it out on me!"

Chloe put the dress and apron on to

a coat hanger and hung them in a small
wardrobe. Then she slid out of Alice's shoes.

"Where are my trainers? Oh, there they
are." Chloe pulled her trainers out from
under the wardrobe, jumping back as
something rushed past her.

"A mouse!" she squealed.

The mouse ran a full
circle round
the room
before darting
back under
the wardrobe.

"Wasn't it sweet?" said Chloe, her eyes
shining. "Did you see its cute little face? It
had the longest whiskers ever. Better not
tell Gerry," she quickly added. "He's the
caretaker. He keeps this place so clean. He's
always sweeping and polishing. He'd have
a fit if he knew there was a mouse."

"I wonder why the mouse is living here," said Blossom thoughtfully. There couldn't be much to eat in the theatre if Gerry kept it so clean. She was about to suggest she went and had a chat with the mouse to see if everything was all right when there was a knock on the dressing-room door.

"Chloe, it's Mum. Are you ready, sweetheart? We've got to rush. I said I'd pick Dad up from the station in ten minutes."

Chloe's face fell.

"I don't want to go yet! We've hardly had any time together," she whispered.

Blossom smiled with pleasure. "I don't want you to go either," she said. "But I promise I'll see you again soon."

"Chloe," called Mum. "Please hurry up."

"Coming," Chloe sighed, and grabbed her bag from the floor. "Bye, Blossom. It was brilliant fun meeting you."

Chloe hurried out to
meet her mother. Blossom
hesitated, wanting to check
on the mouse. Suddenly
she remembered she
hadn't sprinkled Chloe
with magic good-luck
stars and tomorrow
was the first day of the
play.

"Honey mites!" exclaimed Blossom,
swishing the air with her wand. How could
she have been so forgetful? She whizzed
along the corridor hoping to catch Chloe
before she left the theatre. But it was too
late. As Blossom flew into the car park
Chloe and her mum were closing their car
doors. Seconds later the engine purred into
life and the car began to move. Dismayed

Blossom watched it go. Now what? She didn't know where the station was or where Chloe lived. If she was braver, she would have chased after the car, but what if she couldn't keep up and got lost? The thought made Blossom's wings tremble.

"I failed!" she groaned.

It was just as Coral had said it would be. Wings drooping with disappointment, Blossom returned to the Crystal Caves.

# Chapter Four

In the late afternoon sunshine Firefly
Meadow was a glorious blaze of colour
but even the sight of the sycamore tree, its
outstretched branches welcoming Blossom
home, couldn't lift her spirits. Worse still
Coral was sitting near the squirrel hole in
the shade of a cluster of leaves.

"Well?" she said as Blossom landed. "Did
you pass?"

Sadly Blossom shook her head.

"No, I didn't complete my task."

"Told you so," said Coral, smugly

fluttering her orangey-pink wings. "I don't know why Miss Alaska gave you that task when she knew you'd fail."

"What do you mean?" asked Blossom.

Coral narrowed her ice-blue eyes and said spitefully, "Miss Alaska said you wouldn't pass. She didn't think you were brave enough to go through with the task."

"Miss Alaska said that?" exclaimed Blossom.

Coral looked shifty. "Maybe not in those words, but it's what she meant. She said you'd definitely need another day to complete the task. But what if you mess up again? It's the first performance tomorrow. If Chloe doesn't get her good-luck stars, the show will be ruined."

Coral paused to let her words sink in before adding, "I think you should give your task to someone else."

"But that would mean I'd fail," whispered Blossom. "I want to try again."

"Remember the Fairy Bear Promise,"

said Coral sternly. "'I promise to do my best for the *children*', not 'I promise to do my best for myself'."

Blossom twiddled her wand in her paws. Coral was right. Fairy Bears were supposed to put others before themselves. She'd already failed to give Chloe the good luck she needed. What if she didn't succeed a second time? When Blossom looked up, Coral was still staring at her, her blue eyes cold and unfriendly.

Sighing miserably, Blossom headed towards the squirrel hole.

"Where are you going?" called Coral.

Blossom ignored her and flew inside the tree trunk. It was bad enough giving up without sharing the decision with Coral. At first Blossom drifted slowly down the inside of the sycamore tree, delaying the moment when she would have to tell Miss Alaska she couldn't finish her task. But being in the dark was fun, and even though she was feeling sad it made Blossom's fur tingle with pleasure. Her mind drifted to Chloe and suddenly Blossom snapped out of her daydream. There wasn't time to dawdle. School was over for the day. She must catch Miss Alaska before she went home so that she could arrange for another Fairy Bear to take her place. Hoping she wasn't too late, Blossom dived to the bottom of the tree and raced through the Grand Door.

"Please let me get there in time," she muttered, as she flew down the gnarled root staircase and along the Main Tunnel.

The school playground was deserted. Blossom hurried across it and inside the caves. As she neared her class cave, she could hear Miss Alaska talking. Relieved, Blossom slowed, fluttering to the ground.

She leaned against the cave's cool walls to get her breath back. At last she was breathing normally but she couldn't stop her paws and wings from trembling with nerves. Wondering who Miss Alaska was talking to, Blossom peeped into the class cave.

To her surprise Miss Alaska was alone.

"Who's that?" Miss Alaska stopped talking and stared at the doorway.

"It's me," said Blossom, timidly walking into the room.

"Come in," said Miss Alaska, clearly delighted to see her. "I'm rehearsing a speech to give to the new parents of the Fairy Bears who will be joining the school in cub class next term. Would you mind being my audience? It's all very well practising on your own but it's quite another thing speaking in front of others. It makes me nervous just thinking about it."

"*You* get nervous?" Blossom was astonished.

Miss Alaska laughed. "It's quite natural," she said. "Nerves don't have to stop you from doing the things you want to. They can be very useful. If you're  too confident, then you don't always pay attention to what you're doing and you make mistakes."

Blossom sat on her stone seat to listen to Miss Alaska's talk. When she'd finished, Blossom clapped.

"That was very good," she said bashfully. "You didn't look nervous either."

"Thank you, Blossom," Miss Alaska
smiled. "Shall I tell you my secrets for
dealing with nerves? First you must
remember to take long, slow breaths.
When you're nervous, you often take
shallow breaths and that makes you feel
worse. Breathing deeply is very good for
calming the jitters. Next, think to yourself

42

I *can* do this. If you tell yourself you can do something, then you're more likely to succeed. And, lastly, try to enjoy it. Instead of worrying about what might go wrong, think about what will go right."

"That's a lot to remember," said Blossom.

"It's not really," said Miss Alaska kindly. "Deep breaths, think to yourself I can do this and enjoy. It's simple."

Put like that it did sound simple. Blossom's fur crackled with excitement. Perhaps she would be able to complete her task after all.

"How did you get on today?" asked Miss Alaska.

Blossom hesitated. She'd meant to ask Miss Alaska to give her task to someone else but now she wasn't sure what to do. She knew she should put Chloe before herself but she felt more positive of succeeding with Miss Alaska's helpful tips.

"I found Chloe but I didn't manage to give her the good-luck stars," she said.

Miss Alaska smiled. "Finding Chloe was a good start. Have confidence in yourself, Blossom. I wouldn't have given you this job if I didn't think you were ready for it."

Blossom twisted her wand in her paw. Her stomach was fizzing with anxiety. What should she do? She took a deep breath in and let it slowly out. She took another, and another. After a bit her stomach began to calm down.

I can do this, Blossom thought. I know I can.

And it would be fun. Blossom liked Chloe and wanted to help her.

Smiling up at Miss Alaska she said, "Thanks. I won't let you down. Tomorrow

I'm going to finish my task."

Miss Alaska patted Blossom on the shoulder with the tip of her pink and yellow wing.

"That's the spirit," she said. "Blossom the Brave."

# Chapter Five

As she flew home along the cave tunnels, Blossom wondered if she'd made the right decision. But each time she doubted herself she remembered Miss Alaska's delighted face when she'd said she would finish her task. Miss Alaska had great faith in her so she would have faith in herself. Blossom turned off the Main Tunnel and into the one leading to her home cave and was surprised to see Coral. Was she waiting for her? Blossom thought about flying past her but Coral was waving. Reluctantly

Blossom landed beside her.

"Who did Miss Alaska pick to go on the task instead of you?" asked Coral eagerly.

"No one," said Blossom, smiling brightly. "Miss Alaska taught me how to deal with my nerves. I'm carrying on with the task."

Coral folded her wings tightly behind her back and her blue eyes narrowed.

"You," she spluttered. "But . . ."

"I've got to go. It's nearly my tea time," said Blossom, knowing that Coral wasn't happy with her decision. "See you, Coral."

Quickly Blossom stepped round her and flew the short distance home.

That evening Blossom couldn't help worrying about whether she'd made the right decision but she breathed deeply and told herself she had. By bedtime she was exhausted and slept soundly until her alarm clock buzzed her awake early the next morning. There was freshly collected nectar, strawberries and honey biscuits for breakfast. Blossom thought she'd be too anxious to eat but the strawberries were so delicious she managed a whole bowl.

"Good luck," said her mum, hugging

her. "I know you can do this."

Giggling, Blossom wriggled free. It was nice that Miss Alaska and her mum had so much confidence in her. It gave her the courage to prove them right.

The Main Tunnel was very busy. Impatiently Blossom walked behind a large Fairy Bear with enormous red wings. Her stomach was fluttering but she took some deep breaths and felt calmer. Blossom ran her paw along the jewel-studded wall, loving the feel of the magically sparkling gemstones lighting the way. Blossom was nearing the gnarled root staircase when she heard a shout.

"Blossom!"

Turning, she saw Coral a few paces along the Turquoise Tunnel. Blossom waved but Coral seemed upset.

"Please help me," she begged.

## Blossom the Brave

Blossom turned into the tunnel.

"What's wrong?"

"I've lost my wand,"
sobbed Coral. "I must
have dropped it
somewhere."

Blossom stared at
Coral in disbelief.

"Why aren't you at
home?" she asked. "It's far too early for
school."

Coral didn't meet Blossom's eye.

"We'd run out of honey for breakfast.
I've just been to the Nectar Cave to get
some."

The Nectar Cave was a swapping
place where the Fairy Bears traded nectar
for honey with the bees. Blossom wasn't
surprised that Coral's family had run out of
honey. Her parents worked long hours for

King Boris and Queen Tania and Coral was often left to fend for herself. Suddenly Blossom felt sorry for her.

"I'll help you look for your wand," she said kindly.

"Thanks, Blossom," said Coral, immediately cheering up. "I think I dropped it on the way to the nectar cave."

Slowly Coral retraced her paw steps. Blossom walked beside her, keeping her eyes on the tunnel floor, looking for the lost wand.

"It's not here," wailed Coral as they arrived at the nectar cave.

"Maybe someone's picked it up," suggested Blossom. "Let's go in and ask."

There was a queue of Fairy Bears inside the cave.

"The bees haven't arrived yet," explained a motherly-looking Fairy Bear with pretty blue wings.

"We're not here for honey," said
Blossom shyly. "My er . . . my friend was
here earlier and now she's lost her wand."

"Has anyone found a wand?" called the
Fairy Bear. "What colour was it, dear?"

"White," said Coral, sniffing. "With a
gold horseshoe set in its star."

The waiting Fairy Bears shook their heads.

"When did you say you lost it?" called the Fairy Bear at the front of the queue. "Only I've been here for ages and I don't remember seeing you."

"It was quite early," mumbled Coral, a pink flush spreading over her white fur. "Thanks anyway."

As she hurried out of the cave, Blossom stared after her. What was going on? Coral had said she'd been to the Nectar Cave to get honey. But how could she when the bees hadn't arrived yet? With a sinking feeling Blossom realized that Coral didn't have any honey with her. Was this a horrible trick to make her late for her task? At once Blossom rushed outside the cave. Coral was already on her way home.

"Wait!" cried Blossom, flying after her.

54

"What's going on? Have you lost your wand or not?"

Coral's eyes narrowed to mean little slits.

"I just remembered I left my wand at home," she said sweetly. "Silly me!" Thanks for your help, Blossom. I hope I didn't make you too late."

Blossom was so angry! She clenched her paws tightly. The more she thought about Coral's mean trick, the crosser she grew. Blossom took a deep breath. If breathing could help calm nerves, maybe it could help calm her anger too. By her third breath she was beginning to relax. Blossom unclenched her paws.

"Never mind," she said slowly. "Have a good day at *school*. Bye, Coral."

Holding her head high Blossom flew past Coral and made her way as fast as she could to the gnarled root staircase.

# Chapter Six

Blossom flew faster than she'd ever flown in her life. She had to get to the theatre in time. There was no way she was failing her task now. She wanted to pass not just for Chloe's sake but to show Coral that her mean behaviour was a waste of time. Blossom flew over the theatre and straight in through the back door. In a funny way Coral had done her a favour. As Blossom sped down the corridor to Chloe's dressing room, she realized that she hadn't had time to feel nervous. Suddenly Blossom heard footsteps coming down the stairs. She gave an extra burst of speed, meaning to dive into Chloe's dressing room before she was spotted. Then Blossom skidded to a mid-air halt. The door was closed! She'd come within a millimetre of crashing into the green paintwork.

The footsteps were getting closer. Blossom flew to the bottom of the door to see if the gap was wide enough for her to fly underneath but it wasn't. Her heart began to race. Now what? The safest thing would be to stay where she was and hope whoever was coming didn't notice her. Not many humans looked at the ground when they walked. Blossom watched the staircase and soon a foot

appeared in the corridor. It was quickly
followed by another and Blossom squeaked
in alarm!

Gerry the caretaker was working his
way towards her, vigorously polishing the
wooden skirting board with a feather duster
on a long stick. Blossom was seconds from
being swept away. Would Gerry notice her
if she made a sudden dash for the ceiling?
Then miraculously Chloe's door opened
and Chloe, dressed in her blue-and-white
Alice costume, stuck her curly head into the
corridor.

"Er, hello, Gerry. I was just wondering
what that banging sound was."

Chloe quickly shut the door but Blossom
was quicker. She whizzed through it and
landed on Chloe's dressing table where she
collapsed. Her heart was beating furiously
and her wings were trembling.

"Blossom!" Chloe sounded delighted to see her. She lowered her voice to a whisper. "Guess what? The mouse we saw yesterday has babies. There's a nest under my wardrobe. I found it this morning when I first came in. The babies must have been hungry. They were squeaking like mad. They can't stay here. Gerry's bound to find them. I was just checking to see if the coast was clear for me to move the nest. There's a park nearby. It's a much better place for a mouse and her family to live."

"Have you got time to do that now?" asked Blossom. The play would be starting soon.

Chloe checked her watch.

"Yes, if I'm quick," she replied.

"I'll help, then," said Blossom decisively. "But let me talk to the mouse first to explain what's happening."

"You can do that?" Chloe was impressed.

Blossom flew under the wardrobe. It was lovely and dark, and as soon as Blossom's eyes had adjusted she spotted the nest. The mouse crouched in front of it, watching Blossom uneasily with twitching whiskers.

Blossom took a deep breath to help with her own shyness.

"Hello," she said.

"Hello," squeaked the mouse in surprise. "How can you talk to me? I thought only adult Fairy Bears could do that."

61

"Mum and Dad taught me," said Blossom, who loved animals. When she was little she had begged her parents to teach her the magic needed to talk to them. "You're in danger," she continued. "My friend Chloe and I want to help you."

Quickly Blossom explained to the mouse about Gerry the caretaker and Chloe's plan to move her and her family to the park. The mouse was delighted.

"I didn't mean to have my babies here," she explained. "I used to live in a lovely overgrown garden until a family with three cats moved into the house. I was trying to move but got caught in a thunderstorm and came in here to shelter. Then my babies arrived early and I was stuck. They're far too little for me to move them on my own but it's hard living here. It's so clean. There's never enough to eat."

The mouse showed Blossom her three babies. They weren't much larger than Blossom and they all had cute furry faces and long whiskers.

"They're lovely," whispered Blossom.

Proudly the mouse puffed out her chest. "Thank you," she said.

Thoughtfully Blossom made her way back to Chloe. How would they move the nest without damaging it or hurting the babies? The answer came to Blossom in a flash. She flew to Chloe and rested on her hand.

"Can we move the nest in your bag?" she asked.

"Of course," said Chloe. "I'll empty my things out to make more room."

When the bag was empty, Chloe lay on her tummy and stretched her arms under the wardrobe. They were only just long enough to reach the nest. Carefully she pulled it towards her. The mother ran alongside squeaking fretfully. Chloe put the nest in the bottom of her bag then pulled the side down so the mouse could climb in beside it.

"Ready?" she said to Blossom.

Blossom nodded and flew up to the ceiling as Chloe opened her dressing-room door.

The corridor was empty and Chloe hurried along it, holding the bag carefully. As she went outside, a voice made her jump.

"Where are you going in such a hurry?"

Gerry the caretaker was carefully cleaning his duster under the outside tap.

"Hello, Gerry," said Chloe, quickly recovering herself. "I need some fresh air. It's so hot in this costume."

"What's the bag for, then?" Gerry asked curiously.

"The bag . . ." Chloe paused and Blossom, hovering a safe distance away, held her breath. How would Chloe explain the bag away?

"The bag is for my play script and a bottle of water," said Chloe. She gave Gerry a conspiratorial grin. "I'm going to the park to practise my lines. It'll be much quieter there. Every time I try to practise here someone disturbs me."

Gerry grinned. "That's a nice idea. Have you got a watch? You won't be late back?"

"And miss my chance to play Alice?" said Chloe. "I promise I won't be late."

With a cheery wave Chloe set out for the park. Blossom flew high in the sky until the caretaker was out of sight then darted back down to Chloe's side.

"You were brilliant," she said admiringly. "You're a born actress."

"Am I?" Chloe was very pleased. "Then why can't I act in front of an audience? I get so nervous that all my lines fly out of my head."

"Nerves can be a good thing," said Blossom, repeating what Miss Alaska had told her the night before. Carefully carrying the mouse and her nest Chloe listened intently to Blossom as she told her Miss Alaska's tips on dealing with nerves.

"So I have to take deep breaths and keep telling myself I *can* play Alice," said Chloe, when Blossom had finished.

"And enjoy it," Blossom added.

A smile spread slowly across Chloe's face. "It sounds quite simple when you put it like that."

Blossom thought about all she'd achieved by taking control of her nerves.

"It is," she said, grinning back.

# Chapter Seven

The park was a great place for the mouse to live. As soon as Chloe let her out of the bag she ran around squeaking with delight.

"I'd like to live there," the mouse told Blossom. "Under the bush with the yellow flowers. The prickly leaves will keep my nest safe and in the autumn there'll be juicy berries to eat."

Chloe eased the mouse nest out of her bag. It was very fragile and she didn't want to break it. Blossom fluttered beside her interpreting the mouse's squeaks, telling

Chloe exactly where the mouse wanted her nest. Chloe had to lie on her tummy to push the nest far enough under the bush. At last the nest was safely in position, and the mouse couldn't stop thanking everyone.

"Chloe says you're welcome," said Blossom, this time translating human to mouse. "But we have to go now because she's acting in a show."

"Come and visit me," said the mouse.

"We will," promised Blossom.

Chloe stood up and brushed the dirt from her pinafore.

"I'm filthy," she said, pulling a face.

## Blossom the Brave

Chloe was so busy trying to get her apron clean that she forgot to look where she was going. The hem of her dress snagged on a prickly bush and there was loud ripping noise.

"My dress!" she gasped. Her eyes were wide with fright as she took in the torn material. "It's ruined."

Chloe wasn't exaggerating. The white pinafore apron was stained and the blue skirt was ripped. There was no way Chloe could wear it for the performance. Her eyes filled with tears and she sank down on a park bench.

Blossom couldn't bear to see Chloe so unhappy.

"Don't cry," she said, flying down and landing on her hand. "I can fix it."

"How?" Chloe sobbed. "There's not enough time."

"Magic," said Blossom, pointing her wand at Chloe's dress.

"Really?"

Chloe brushed her tears away. "Oh, Blossom, can you do that?" she asked hopefully.

"Yes," said Blossom, trying to sound confident. Mending Chloe's dress would take a lot of skill. Was she able to perform such strong magic? As Blossom pointed her wand at Chloe's dress, her paw was shaking and she had to grip the wand tightly to stop herself from dropping it. Blossom mumbled:

## Blossom the Brave

*"Wand repair*
*This horrible tear."*

The wand twitched and Blossom gripped
it more tightly but only a few small pink
stars plopped from its tip. The stars drifted
towards Chloe's torn dress but evaporated
before they reached it. Blossom gritted her
teeth, and repeated:

*"Wand repair*
*This horrible tear."*

The wand made a soft hissing sound but
this time there weren't any stars. In a panic
Blossom waved the wand wildly at Chloe's
costume, and chanted:

*"Repair, repair, repair,*
*This horrible, horrible tear."*

Nothing! The wand lay lifeless in Blossom's trembling paw. Blossom's tummy was churning so badly it was making her feel sick. Why wasn't her magic working? Then she remembered what Miss Alaska had said yesterday.

"Nerves are awful. They can stop you doing something you want to."

Was that it? Were Blossom's nerves stopping her magic from working? Blossom shook her wings. She took several long deep breaths and felt better. With a slightly trembling paw she pointed her wand at Chloe's dress and said firmly:

> "*Wand repair*
> *This horrible tear.*"

The wand jerked, its handle grew warm, there was a loud whooshing sound and a

fountain of pink stars flowed from its tip
and cascaded over Chloe. The blue fabric
began to glitter. More stars poured from
Blossom's wand until Chloe's dress was
crackling with magic.

> *"Make the apron clean and bright,*
> *From dirty brown to sparkling white,"*

Blossom sang confidently.

Gradually the fizzing stopped and the
glittering stars faded away. Chloe jumped
up and gave a twirl.

"It worked," she gasped. "The magic
worked. Blossom, you're brilliant!"

Blossom grinned.

"And you're going to be too," she said.
"Come on, Chloe. It's time for you to play
Alice."

Back in Chloe's dressing room Blossom

perched on the mirror while Chloe yanked a comb through her hair.

"Shame you couldn't fix this for me," she joked. "It's full of twigs from the bushes in the park."

"Maybe next time," said Blossom, who was quite exhausted from performing such a strong spell.

"Does that mean I get to see you again?" asked Chloe.

"I hope so." Blossom had grown very fond of her new friend. Rallying herself she stood up. There were still two things she had to do. First she had to sprinkle Chloe with good-luck magic, even though Blossom knew she didn't need it any more. Blossom waved her wand, loving the warmth of it glowing in her hand as she chanted her spell.

*"Good luck to Chloe and everyone.*
*Make their show lots of fun."*

Pink stars fell gently over Chloe, making
her hair and skin sparkle. Chloe put out her
hands to catch them, laughing delightedly
as they fizzled away.

"Thank you, Blossom!" she cried.

"And here's something to remember me
by," said Blossom, concentrating on her
next spell:

*"From me to you,*
*A star that's true."*

The wand jerked
as a large pink
star suddenly
burst from its end.
Catching it in both

78

paws Blossom held out the star to Chloe.

"A friendship star," she said, smiling.

Chloe's green eyes shone with delight.

"It's beautiful," she whispered, carefully putting the star in the pocket of her apron. I'll always remember you, Blossom. And this star will bring me extra luck when I play Alice."

Blossom laughed. "You're going to be fantastic," she said.

Blossom stayed to watch the opening of the play. Chloe was amazing. She didn't seem nervous at all. Blossom could tell she was enjoying herself!

The little Fairy Bear wanted to watch the whole play but she had to get back to school to tell Miss Alaska she'd completed her task. Flying away from the theatre, Blossom was so excited at her own success she turned a series of cartwheels.

"Watch where you're going," cried a butterfly, swerving to avoid a collision.

"Sorry!" said Blossom, quickly righting herself.

She sped home, skimming across Firefly Meadow then soaring up high to reach the squirrel hole hidden in the branches of the sycamore tree. Blossom dived through the hole and floated down the tree's dark insides. She hopped through the Grand Door and jumped down the gnarled root staircase two steps at a time. She arrived back in class panting but happy.

"Blossom's here," called Sparkle excitedly as her friend entered the cave.

Everyone stopped tidying up and stared at Blossom as she made her way to the front of the class. Blossom held her head high, smiling at everyone, even Coral who glared nastily at her as she passed.

## Blossom the Brave

"Hello, Blossom," said Miss Alaska. "I can tell from your face that it's good news."

"I completed my task," agreed Blossom proudly.

The class cheered noisily and clapped their wings together. When they'd calmed down, Blossom told everyone about her exciting day. Then Miss Alaska stepped forward.

"Blossom is not only clever and brave,"

she announced. "She is also very modest.
I don't expect many of you knew before
today that she can speak with animals, even
though it's an advanced skill usually learned
in the seniors. I'm very proud of you,
Blossom. Class, let's give Blossom the Fairy
Bear Salute."

Blossom's pale-gold fur turned scarlet
with embarrassment. The Fairy Bear Salute
was only given on very special occasions.

"Deep breath," whispered Miss Alaska,
winking at her.

"And enjoy it," Blossom whispered back.

The little Fairy Bear breathed deeply,
and as the class dipped their wings she *did*
enjoy it!

# Blossom

1. Favourite colour – *pink*

   2. Favourite gemstone – *pink diamond*

3. Best flower – *pansy*

   4. Cutest animal – *mouse*

5. Birthday month – *May*

   6. Yummiest food – *honey biscuits*

7. Favourite place – *Diamond Dell*

   8. Hobbies – *thinking up stories, talking to animals*

9. Best ever season – *spring*

   10. Worst thing – *cruelty to animals*

# Sparkle Saves the Day

# Chapter One

Sparkle was about to enter her class cave when another Fairy Bear with brightly glittering wings fluttered past. Hardly able to believe her eyes, Sparkle stopped. She would do anything for wings like that! Impulsively she called out, "You look beautiful. How did you make your wings glitter?"

The Fairy Bear turned round and Sparkle held her breath, recognizing her as an older Fairy Bear called April. Would she be too grand to speak to a mere junior like herself? April smiled then modestly fluttered her wings.

"Thank you. Mum stuck jewels on my wings with magic for a birthday treat."

Sparkle stared at April's twinkling wings until she reached the end of the tunnel and disappeared round the corner.

"Hello, Sparkle, what are you doing out here? Hurry up inside. I'm sending someone on their first task today," said Miss Alaska as she swept past Sparkle and entered the class cave. Eagerly Sparkle followed her.

## Sparkle Saves the Day

Fairy Bears started taking tasks in the last year of juniors and had to pass them all before they were allowed to move up to the senior classes. The tasks were really important and usually involved helping someone or the environment they lived in. Sparkle hadn't done any tasks yet and was longing to go out on her first one.

Please let Miss Alaska choose me, she thought as she sat down next to her friend Blossom.

"Hello," whispered Blossom. "You were almost late."

"I know," said Sparkle, putting her wand on the table and neatly closing her red wings. "Guess what I saw!"

Blossom put a paw to her lips shushing Sparkle as Miss Alaska started to call the register. Sparkle wriggled impatiently. She wanted to tell Blossom about April's wings.

When Miss Alaska had finished, she held up a large green sycamore leaf. An excited murmur rippled round the class and Sparkle sat up straight, April's wings suddenly forgotten.

"It's task time again," said Miss Alaska. "But first let's say the Fairy Bear Promise."

Stones scraped on the class cave floor as the Fairy Bears stood up and joined paws. Sparkle had Blossom on one side of her and Primrose on the other. Excitedly she clutched their paws. Would it be her turn to go out on a task? She hoped so!

"I promise to do my best. I promise to work hard to care for the world and all its plants, animals and children. This is the Fairy Bear Promise," Sparkle chanted earnestly. She stared at Miss Alaska, hoping she would be chosen.

Miss Alaska looked at the sycamore leaf.

"This task is for Sparkle," she announced.

Wings trembling with delight, Sparkle took the leaf to find out what her task was.

"Guess what!" she said, her brown eyes shining as she read the task. "I'm to help a colony of butterflies. They're living on a piece of wasteland in the middle of a town, but developers are about to build houses on it so they need to find a new home."

At the bottom of the task was a map. The town was a long way from the sycamore tree. Sparkle couldn't believe her good luck. She loved pretty creatures like butterflies and she loved flying too.

"Poor you," said Coral, who was known for her sharp tongue. "The beautiful butterflies will make you look quite plain, Sparkle."

Sparkle's wings drooped and she stared at Coral in dismay.

"The tasks are about helping others, Coral," said Miss Alaska sternly. "Sparkle isn't plain but she'll be too busy helping the butterflies to worry about her looks."

The class giggled, knowing that Sparkle was very particular about her appearance. Her fur shone from constant combing and she loved pretty things. As Sparkle walked to the door, she sneaked a look in the magic mirror. At first a pretty bear with gleaming gold fur and bright red wings stared back. Then in a swirl of silver the picture changed. Sparkle held her breath, wondering what she would see next. The magic mirror didn't always show reflections. Sometimes it showed things that were magical or useful. As the new picture became clearer, Sparkle saw an overgrown patch of land bursting with wildflowers and butterflies.

"Oh," she sighed, leaning closer so her nose almost touched the mirror's surface. "They're beautiful."

In a flash of silver the butterflies were replaced by a picture of a grimy street littered with empty food wrappers and drinks cans. Sparkle gasped at the contrast. This road was horrible. A stream of cars rumbled alongside the pavement where an athletic-looking girl was walking. Her light brown hair was held back by a brightly-coloured headband with *Isabel* stitched across the top. Her shoulders were bent with the weight of the large school bag she carried on her back.

"Poor Isabel," murmured Sparkle. "I'm not surprised she looks fed up."

Sparkle loved children and was disappointed that her task wasn't to help Isabel. But the mirror was changing again and Isabel was replaced by the butterflies. Captivated, Sparkle soon forgot Isabel as she watched the butterflies dancing in the air. As the picture faded away, Sparkle sighed. It didn't matter that Miss Alaska had said that tasks were about helping others – the beautiful butterflies still made her feel plain. Sadly she wrapped the sycamore leaf with her task written on round her wand and flew from the class cave. Sparkle was halfway across the playground when a wonderful idea occurred to her. Flying faster, she headed home.

# Chapter Two

"Mum," called Sparkle, rushing indoors. "Can I borrow your diamonds?"

The Crystal Caves were full of sparkling jewels. Fairy Bears used them to decorate their homes on special occasions. Sparkle's mum was very fond of diamonds and had a large collection.

"Hello, dear." Sparkle's grandma poked her head out of the living cave.

"Grandma," squealed Sparkle, rushing forward and hugging her. "What a lovely surprise."

## Sparkle Saves the Day

"And for me too," said Grandma, her silver wings quivering with delight. "Your mum asked me to look after Fizz while she popped out. Why aren't you at school?"

"I'm going on my first task," said Sparkle. Excitedly she told Grandma about

the butterflies, adding, "I came home to ask Mum if I could borrow her diamonds to make my wings look pretty. Can I, Grandma? Will you stick them to my wings for me?"

Grandma's face clouded. "I don't know, Sparkle. They're not mine to lend."

"Please, Grandma. Mum often lets me borrow her things," Sparkle begged.

"Mummy lend 'Parkle diamonds," said Fizz, tottering towards her big sister.

Sparkle held her breath. It sounded like Fizz was saying that Mum had lent Sparkle the diamonds before. Grandma hesitated. "Please, 'Anma," said Fizz. "Mummy let 'Parkle."

"Well, if you're sure Mum won't mind, then you can," she said eventually.

"Thanks!" squealed Sparkle, hugging Grandma then scooping up Fizz to hug her

98

too. "I promise I'll look after them. Will you stick them on for me?"

It took much longer than Sparkle had thought to magically stick her mum's diamonds to her wings but when Grandma had finished they both agreed it was worth the effort. Grandma made Sparkle do a twirl.

"You look beautiful," she sighed.

"Pretty 'Parkle," cooed Fizz, clapping her paws in delight.

"I can't wait to meet the butterflies," said Sparkle happily. They would have to like her now!

Unused to the extra weight of the diamonds, Sparkle held her wings stiffly as she flew to the Grand Door. It was mid-morning so the tunnels were empty. Sparkle was disappointed that there was no one to see her but relieved that she hadn't been caught in the early morning crush, as that might have ruined her wings. The Grand Door was closed. After climbing the gnarled root staircase, Sparkle reached for the leaf-shaped door handle. Twisting it round, she pushed the door open and stepped inside the tree trunk. The diamonds on Sparkle's wings twinkled magically in the dark. Sparkle was ecstatic.

"I want diamonds on my wings every day!" she exclaimed.

Excitedly Sparkle leaped into the air. She loved the way the jewels made her wings glitter and was so busy admiring them she

nearly flew past the squirrel hole. Stopping
with a jerk, Sparkle anxiously checked that
all her mum's diamonds were still in place.
Satisfied she hadn't lost any, Sparkle flew
outside and landed on a branch to study her
map.

At first Sparkle enjoyed her long flight to
town. The sunlight made her wings shine
more brightly than usual and she saw two
butterflies and a bumblebee stare at her as
she flew by. She was surprised when she
tired more quickly than usual but soon
realized it was the diamonds making her
wings feel heavy.

"Not far now," said Sparkle firmly,
resisting the urge to stop for a rest.

She was very glad when the landscape
changed from neat green fields to sprawling
rows of houses. Sparkle flew down to a
street lamp and perched on the top to check

her map again. It was such a relief to rest her wings that Sparkle studied the map for longer than she needed to. At last it was time to go. Rolling the sycamore leaf back round her wand, Sparkle set off on the final part of her journey. She flew over a school, its playground crowded with noisy children, and there on the corner of the next street was an overgrown patch of land.

"That's it!" cried Sparkle.

Quickly she flew along the street. It was as dirty and noisy as the one she'd seen in the magic mirror. Sparkle shuddered, wishing that her task could have been somewhere nicer. At the corner she flew between two sprawling bushes and into the wasteland then stopped in surprise. It was lovely here. Hidden from the road by overgrown bushes, the area was a riot of coloured wildflowers, nettles and bushes.

## Sparkle Saves the Day

Sparkle breathed deeply, enjoying the sweet scent of nectar as she hovered overhead. The flowers were twitching and fluttering as if they'd magically come to life. Sparkle stared, then realized that it wasn't the flowers moving. It was butterflies. They were everywhere, darting from plant to plant on their beautiful wings.

Suddenly Sparkle was overcome with shyness. The butterflies were much bigger than her and they were all so pretty. Nervously she ran a paw through her fur and then checked her wings. The diamonds flashed miniature rainbows in the sunlight, making Sparkle's red wings twinkle. She flushed with pleasure.

Reassured that she looked good enough to meet the butterflies, Sparkle flew down and landed on a yellow-headed daisy. It smelt delicious. Thirsty after her long

flight, Sparkle had a long drink of nectar.
A butterfly with red wings and four brightly
coloured spots landed nearby. It was about
to drink some nectar when it noticed
Sparkle's diamonds. One of its antennae
twitched in surprise. Shyly Sparkle dipped
a wing. The butterfly dipped a wing back
then fluttered closer. Sparkle did a slow
twirl, so the beautiful butterfly could see

how pretty her wings were. The butterfly clicked a greeting.

"Hello," Sparkle softly answered.

Another butterfly with bright blue wings edged with black and white flew over. She was followed by an orange butterfly, with pretty black and blue markings. Soon the air was alive with butterflies, crowding round Sparkle. She basked in all the attention until a pearly white butterfly cheekily tapped his enormous wing against hers. Sparkle wished she could understand the butterfly, but talking to animals wasn't taught until the seniors.

"Plink?" she asked, thinking of the chasing game they played at home.

The butterfly tapped Sparkle again then slowly flew away, checking to see she was following. Satisfied that she was, the butterfly sped up, dipping and diving each time Sparkle tried to tap him back. The other butterflies joined in and Sparkle raced through the air with them, sometimes chasing and sometimes being chased. This was the best game of Plink she'd played in ages! The butterflies were fast and Sparkle had to work hard to keep up with them. Eventually Sparkle sank down on the soft head of a purple knapweed to get her breath back and have another drink.

"Truce," she panted.

Quizzically a blue butterfly landed next to her. Sparkle rested her head on her paw, closing her eyes to show the butterfly she was tired. Something fell to the ground with a chink. Sparkle opened her eyes. What was that? The blue butterfly pointed his antennae at her wing. Thinking he was admiring her again, Sparkle dipped her wings back.

"Thank you," she said.

## Sparkle Saves the Day

The butterfly shook his head and
pointed his antennae
again.

Sparkle peered
over her shoulder at
her wings.

"Oh no!" she
gasped.

Where had all Mum's
diamonds gone? Sparkle
tried to count the diamonds left on her
wings. From the gaps she guessed she'd lost
half of her mum's precious jewels.

# Chapter Three

Sparkle's wings went ice cold. She'd promised to be careful with the diamonds and now she'd lost them. Mum would be furious. And what about Grandma? Would she be in trouble too? The blue butterfly was tapping his wing against Sparkle's as if he wanted her to follow him. Sparkle flew after him to the ground and there under the knapweed was a diamond. Gratefully she pounced on it.

"Thank you," she said.

The blue butterfly nodded his head then

called out to his friends. Immediately the butterflies stopped chasing each other and crowded round. The butterfly spoke to his friends in clicks and squeaks then they all began searching for the missing diamonds. Each time they found a diamond the butterfly tapped Sparkle on the wing and showed her where it was. Sparkle couldn't hold all the diamonds in her paws and look for more at the same time so she made a pile under a bush.

The butterflies searched for ages until there were only a few diamonds left to find. Eventually they drifted away until only the blue butterfly was left. Sparkle flew alongside him, searching the remaining patch of ground. Where were the last few diamonds? She had to find them quickly so that she could start on her task. Sparkle had been so busy having fun she'd forgotten that the butterflies were about to lose their home.

Suddenly everything went black. Sparkle's heart thumped wildly as she spun through the air, trapped inside a cave with soft, warm walls. This was terrifying. What had happened to her? Then the walls of the cave opened. As the light poured in, Sparkle waited for a chance to escape, but a girl's voice whispered, "Hello. Are you some kind of fairy?"

With a start Sparkle realized she was standing on a girl's cupped hand. The girl was staring at her with amazement. Sparkle stared back, taking in her light brown hair held back with a hairband. She knew this girl. It was Isabel, from the picture in the magic mirror.

"Hello, Isabel," said Sparkle. "I'm not a fairy – I'm a Fairy Bear."

"A Fairy Bear!"
Isabel's pale blue
eyes popped with
excitement. "How
do you know my
name?" she asked.

Smiling shyly
Sparkle pointed
to Isabel's
headband.
Isabel
chuckled
then said,
"Do you
live here?
How come
I've never seen
you before? I've come here every day on
my way home from school since we moved.
We used to live in the country, but then

III

Dad lost his job and he could only find a new one in town. Mum's got a new job too. It's lonely going home to an empty house. That's why I come here. This patch of land reminds me of our old home." Isabel stopped talking and blushed. "Sorry, I always talk too much."

"I'm here to help the butterflies," said Sparkle. "This land is going to be built on so I have to find the butterflies a new home."

Isabel's face fell.

"I heard about that from Dad. I've been trying not to think about it. Where are you going to move the butterflies to?"

Sparkle's wings quivered sadly.

"I'm not sure yet. I've lost some things that didn't belong to me and I have to find them before I can help the butterflies."

"I'm good at looking for things," said

Isabel eagerly. "What have you lost?"

"My mum's diamonds," said Sparkle.

"Diamonds!" Isabel was shocked and impressed. "Your mum let you borrow her diamonds?"

"Sort of," said Sparkle. She stared at her paws, suddenly ashamed of herself. She hadn't been exactly truthful when she'd persuaded Grandma to let her take the jewels.

"Where do you think you lost them?" said Isabel, dumping her school bag on the ground.

Isabel was very thorough. With her eyes glued to the ground she walked in a line across the patch of wasteland, then, reaching the end, walked back. Up and down she went, bending each time she spotted something glittering in the sunlight.

"They're so tiny," she said, staring at the

miniature diamond in her cupped hand.

There were lots of false alarms but Isabel kept searching until all the diamonds had been recovered. Sparkle couldn't stop thanking her.

## Sparkle Saves the Day

"How are you going to get them home –
do you have a bag?" asked Isabel. She
stared at the pile of jewels glittering in the
sunlight.

Sparkle hadn't thought about that. There
was no way she could magically stick the
jewels back on her wings without help.
She could just about carry them but it
would make flying difficult and what if she
accidentally dropped one? She did need a
bag.

Thoughtfully Sparkle twiddled her wand;
it was very pretty, gold in colour with a
cluster of tiny red rubies set in the star.
Sparkle was good at magic but she couldn't
magic up a bag from nothing. Maybe there
was something on the wasteland she could
use to make a bag from . . . She stared
around but the only thing she could see was
Isabel's enormous school bag. It was perfect!

She could easily shrink that to Fairy Bear size if Isabel would lend it to her.

"Where do you live?" asked Isabel. "Can I help you to carry the diamonds home?"

Sparkle didn't answer. She was having a brilliant idea. It meant trusting Isabel but Sparkle sensed that she would be good at keeping secrets.

Wings trembling with excitement, she said, "I live in the Crystal Caves. It's a long way from here. If you really don't mind helping me take the diamonds home, then you could visit. It would mean shrinking you down to my size, though."

"R–r–really?" stuttered Isabel, her pale blue eyes shining. "Would I have wings as well?"

Isabel's enthusiasm was catching and made Sparkle laugh.

"Of course," she said.

# Sparkle Saves the Day

"Go on, then." Isabel stood very still. "Shrink me now."

"Hold on to your bag," said Sparkle. "We'll need it to carry the diamonds back and I'm not sure if I can do two shrinking spells in a row."

Isabel snatched up her bag as Sparkle experimentally waved her wand. The cluster of rubies flashed in the sunlight as Sparkle chanted:

> "*Shrink Isabel down as small as a bee*
> *Then give her wings just like me.*"

The wand trembled. Sparkle held her breath. It was a complicated spell. Would she have enough energy to make the magic work?

# Chapter Four

The wand vibrated, slowly at first then faster and faster. The cluster of rubies glowed and the gold star shone like the sun. Sparkle gripped the wand tightly as with a loud pop a river of sparkling red stars burst from its tip. They rained over Isabel, making her skin and hair glitter.

"Oh!" squeaked Isabel, her eyes widening. "I feel funny."

Isabel was shrinking. Her voice faded as her body became tinier. Red stars popped and fizzed at Isabel's back then disappeared in a glittering swirl of red. Sparkle clapped her paws with delight. That had been hard work but she'd done it! She'd shrunk Isabel to the same size as herself. For a moment no one spoke then the tiny Isabel threw herself at Sparkle and hugged her tight.

"Thank you," she gabbled. "Just look at me. I'm like a fairy. Look at my lovely wings."

Isabel twirled round, showing off the beautiful butterfly-shaped wings sprouting from her back.

"They're the same colour as yours," she said proudly.

"Almost," said Sparkle enviously, noticing that Isabel's wings had streaks of gold that shimmered in the sunlight.

Frowning with concentration, Isabel fluttered her wings. "I can fly!" she cried.

"Look, Sparkle, I'm flying!"

"Well done." Sparkle clapped loudly as Isabel flew in a circle. "Take bigger wing strokes. That's it, now you're not wobbling!"

"This is brilliant fun," cried Isabel, changing direction.

"Are you ready to fly home with me or do you want more practice?" asked Sparkle.

"Let's go now," said Isabel. Confidently she landed next to Sparkle and together they placed the diamonds safely in the bag.

"I can't wait to see your home!" said Isabel excitedly.

Sparkle and Isabel flew side by side, carrying Isabel's bag between them.

"Flying is brilliant," said Isabel, her eyes sparkling, as they flew over the green

countryside. As Firefly Meadow drew closer Sparkle felt a sharp pang of worry. What would Mum say when she returned the diamonds? Would she be cross with Sparkle for persuading Grandma to let her take them? And what about her task? She hadn't even started it yet! Sparkle suddenly felt very guilty.

Approaching the sycamore tree, Sparkle

saw two Fairy Bears sitting amongst its leaves. She was relieved that they were too busy talking to notice her new friend fly in through the squirrel hole. Suddenly Sparkle was worried about bringing Isabel back to the Crystal Caves. It wasn't something that happened very often. All Sparkle wanted to do was return Mum's diamonds and get started with her task.

Sparkle held on to Isabel's hand as they flew in the darkness to the bottom of the tree but Isabel wasn't scared of the dark.

"This is brilliant," sighed Isabel. "It reminds me of night-time in the country. It doesn't get properly dark in the town because of all the street lights."

Isabel was amazed by the Grand Door.

"It's enormous," she cried. "And I love the leaf-shaped handle."

They flew down the gnarled root staircase

124

and along the main tunnel.

"Slower!" begged Isabel, gazing with
awe at the glittering walls.

Sparkle laughed as she slowed down. She
was anxious to return her mum's diamonds
but it was such fun sharing her home with
Isabel. It made her see the Crystal Caves
with new eyes. Suddenly she was very
glad she lived in such an amazing place.
At the diamond archway that marked
the entrance to the Royal Tunnel Isabel
stopped in mid-air.

"That's so beautiful," she gasped.
"Where does it lead to?"

Sparkle hesitated. The Royal Tunnel
led to the Royal Caves, home of King
Boris and Queen Tania. Fairy Bears were
allowed as far as the spectacular Butterfly
Bridge that crossed the underground stream.
It was one of the prettiest places in the

Crystal Caves and Sparkle longed to show Isabel. Deciding the diamonds would be safe in Isabel's bag for a while longer, she made a detour under the archway.

"That's the most amazing bridge I've ever seen," said Isabel, unable to take her eyes off the jewel-studded bridge shaped like a butterfly.

The stream gurgled cheerfully beneath the bridge. Isabel sat on the bank and dipped her hands in the crystal-clear water.

"Careful you don't get your wings wet," warned Sparkle. "It's impossible to fly with wet wings."

"This reminds me of my old home," said Isabel wistfully. "We had a stream at the bottom of our garden. We've hardly got any garden now. Half of it is patio and the rest is scrubby grass with a border of weeds.

126

Mum and Dad keep saying they'll tidy it up but they're always too busy working."

"Maybe you could do it for them," suggested Sparkle.

Isabel let her hand drift in the ice-cold water.

"Perhaps," she said thoughtfully.

It wasn't far from the Royal Tunnel to Sparkle's cave but it took ages to get there. Isabel kept stopping to admire the jewels in the walls and Isabel begged Sparkle to take her to see the school caves. The Fairy Bears were all in lessons so Sparkle took Isabel for a quick fly round the empty playground.

"I'd love to go inside the class caves," said Isabel longingly.

"That would give everyone a surprise," giggled Sparkle.

As they were leaving the school, Isabel

spotted the entrance to the Crystal Maze on the opposite side of the tunnel and flitted over.

"Don't go in," warned Sparkle, hurrying after her. "If you take a wrong turning, you'll be lost inside for ages."

"It's beautiful," sighed Isabel, reaching out to touch the colourful column of crystal decorating the maze's entrance.

Sparkle couldn't help laughing at Isabel's excitement.

"You're a bad influence," she joked. "Mum's always complaining that I'm easily distracted and you're making me worse. Come on, I have to take these diamonds back before I lose them again."

Reluctantly Isabel left the Crystal Maze and followed Sparkle. As they grew nearer to Sparkle's home, Isabel fell silent as if lost in her thoughts.

"We're here," said Sparkle, hesitating at her front door.

Isabel hovered beside her. "Look at your front door. It's so pretty. Do all doors have jewels on them?"

Sparkle nodded. "Every door is different."

"Our old house had a name, Bracken Cottage, but our new house has a boring old number," said Isabel wistfully.

Now that the moment had come to return Mum's diamonds Sparkle was very nervous.

"Would you mind waiting here?" she asked Isabel. "In case Mum's cross with me."

"Of course I don't mind," said Isabel. "Shall I wait in that tiny cave over there?"

"That's a great idea," said Sparkle, relieved that Isabel wasn't upset.

## Sparkle Saves the Day

Isabel emptied the diamonds out of
her school bag and into Sparkle's arms,
then hurried along the tunnel to the cave.
Hugging the diamonds
close to her chest,
Sparkle
carried them
indoors.

"Hello,"
she called out.
"Is anyone
home?"

Her heart was
banging nervously. Would
Mum tell her and Grandma off for taking
the diamonds?

"Shhh!" whispered Grandma, appearing
from Fizz's cave. "Your sister has just fallen
asleep."

"Grandma!" whispered Sparkle, relieved

that her mum wasn't back yet. She hung her head, staring at her paws. "I've got something to tell you."

"You've lost some of your mum's diamonds," said Grandma flatly.

"I did lose some but I found them again. But I wasn't very honest. Mum has never lent me her diamonds before."

Wordlessly Grandma reached out and took the diamonds from Sparkle.

"I'm sorry," Sparkle whispered, her red wings drooping miserably.

Surprisingly Grandma smiled.

"That wasn't a nice thing to do, but I'm pleased you realized your mistake and had the courage to own up." She reached out and softly stroked Sparkle's wing with her own silver one.

"Come on," she said kindly. "Let's put the diamonds away before Mum gets back.

I know you won't do this again. You've learned your lesson."

# Chapter Five

Sparkle and Isabel flew out of the squirrel hole and across Firefly Meadow.

"I don't want this to end," said Isabel, flying slower. "I love the Crystal Caves and I love flying."

"Your parents would miss you if you didn't go back," said Sparkle, swerving to avoid colliding with a wasp.

"Ugh!" shuddered Isabel. "That wasp was enormous! Maybe there are advantages to being big. And, yes, my parents would miss me. I'd miss them too."

She checked her watch and sighed.

"We'll have to hurry. Mum and Dad will be back from work soon."

"I can't wait to see where you live," said Sparkle.

"It's not as exciting as your home," said Isabel. "It's on a busy road and the garden's tiny."

Soon Sparkle saw exactly what Isabel meant. She lived in a tall house with wide stone steps leading straight up from the pavement. Small patio pots containing half-dead weeds were arranged on either side of the stairs and empty window boxes hung from the downstairs windows. As they approached the house, Isabel began to giggle.

"We'll have to fly over the side gate and into the back garden," she said. "I can't get in until you turn me back to my proper size.

Look at my front-door key. It won't fit the
lock any more."

Isabel reached inside her school polo shirt
and pulled out a piece of ribbon hanging
round her neck. Dangling from the ribbon
was a tiny silver key.

"Whoops!" chuckled Sparkle. "I forgot you use keys. We use magic to lock our front doors."

"That's so cool," Isabel sighed.

Isabel's back garden was exactly as she'd described it. Sparkle could see why Isabel stopped off at the patch of wasteland every day. It was much prettier there. She landed in the far corner next to a tiny garden shed and Isabel reluctantly landed beside her.

"That was so much fun," she said.

Sparkle pointed her wand at Isabel.

"Ready?"

"I suppose so," said Isabel, fluttering her red-gold wings one last time.

Waving her wand Sparkle chanted:

*"Wand before my very eyes
Return Isabel to her proper size."*

The wand trembled. Sparkle held on tight as a stream of glittering red stars shot out from the end, covering Isabel.

"Ooh!" Isabel squealed. "That tickles!"

She giggled as the stars fizzled away on her skin, her voice growing louder as she returned to her normal height.

"Phew!" she said when the magic had finished. "Thank goodness the magic knew when to stop or I might have ended up like a giant."

In the distance a door slammed and Isabel said, "Sounds like my mum's home. The time after school normally drags, but not today. It's flown!" she added, chuckling at her own joke.

The back door opened and a tired-looking lady wearing a crumpled suit poked her head out.

"There you are, Isabel. How did you get

into the garden without unlocking the back
door?"

"Hi, Mum. I came in through the side
gate," said Isabel truthfully. "I have to go,"
she whispered to Sparkle. "Thanks for a
brilliant time. I hope I see you again soon."

As Isabel hurried indoors, Sparkle took
another look around her garden. Poor
Isabel! It must be hard for her to settle here
when she was used to open countryside.

"Honey mites!" exclaimed Sparkle
suddenly. The butterflies! She had to help
them before they became homeless and
she failed her task. But it was too late to
do anything now. It was early evening.
Sparkle had to go home before dark or she
would fail her task anyway. Quickly she
flew back to the Crystal Caves, wondering
how to help the butterflies. The only thing
she could think of was to persuade them

to move to the country. But somehow that didn't feel like the right solution. Arriving back at the Crystal Caves, Sparkle was surprised to see Miss Alaska waiting for her at the bottom of the gnarled root staircase.

"Hello, Sparkle. How did you get on?"

Sparkle hesitated. She'd had a great time playing with the butterflies, meeting Isabel and showing her the Crystal Caves, but she didn't think Miss Alaska would be interested in hearing about that.

"I found the butterflies," she said, "but I'm not sure how to help them."

"Hmmm," said Miss Alaska, writing something in her leaf note book. "Did something distract you from your task?"

Sparkle flushed. "There's nowhere to move the butterflies to," she answered, avoiding the question. "The town is so dirty and ugly."

"Is it?" Miss Alaska sounded surprised. "Have you explored it properly? Looks aren't everything, Sparkle. You need to find out what things are like on the inside. I suggest that tomorrow you stop fussing about appearances and get on with the job."

Sparkle's wings twitched uncomfortably as Miss Alaska fixed her with a long stare. It was a good thing she didn't know about the diamonds or she would have been even crosser.

"I will," she whispered, promising herself that tomorrow would be different.

The following morning Sparkle left the Crystal Caves early and flew to town.

Instead of going to visit the butterflies she decided that first she would find a new home for them. Remembering how thorough Isabel had been when searching for the lost diamonds Sparkle followed her example, flying up and down the streets, looking for somewhere for the butterflies to live.

There were a couple more patches of wasteland but Sparkle didn't want to move the butterflies there in case that land was also going to be built on soon. She found a play park but there were no plants, just play equipment and benches for people to sit on. Its bareness reminded Sparkle of Isabel's garden and it gave her an idea.

She fluttered down and rested on the top of the swings while she thought it through. If her plan worked, it would be good for both the butterflies and Isabel. Sparkle couldn't wait to put her plan into action, but first she needed Isabel's permission.

Excitedly she flew towards the wasteland to wait for Isabel to visit. But as she got closer a small doubt began to nag at her. What if Isabel didn't stop off at the wasteland on her way home from school? Sparkle couldn't leave it to chance. The builders might start work any day. She had to speak to Isabel before it was too late! Then she had another good idea. Isabel had visited Sparkle's school, so why didn't she visit Isabel at hers?

# Chapter Six

Arriving at Isabel's school, Sparkle was surprised to see a crowd of adults outside the gates. She hadn't realized it was home time already. She looked around for somewhere to wait for Isabel and found a metal school sign to perch on. Seconds later a sea of red-and-grey clothed children streamed out of the school buildings. Sparkle leaned forward, trying to spot Isabel. There! Eagerly she flew towards the mousey-haired girl. But it wasn't Isabel, and the girl screamed and flapped at Sparkle, thinking she was a bee.

"Stay calm," called a parent. "Look, the bee's flying away."

"Too right!" yelped Sparkle, speeding in the opposite direction.

"Eeek!" squealed a boy, swatting her as she flew past. "It tried to sting me."

Sparkle was too frightened to be indignant. Her wings were trembling so badly she could hardly fly.

"Sparkle," hissed a voice. "Over here."

Isabel! Relieved Sparkle dashed towards her friend and, landing on her shoulder, hid under her hair.

Isabel quickened her pace, leaving behind the noisy children.

"You can come out now," she said, once they were safely on the wasteland.

"Thanks." Sparkle fluttered out of hiding and rested on Isabel's hand.

Isabel's cheeks turned pink with pleasure.

"How come everyone thought you were a bee?" she giggled.

Sparkle combed her ruffled fur.

"We're the same size, we're both furry and we both have wings. It's an easy mistake to make if you don't believe in magic."

"How can you not believe in magic?" Isabel exclaimed.

"I know!" said Sparkle indignantly.

They laughed together until Isabel said curiously, "What were you doing at my school? Were you waiting for me?"

"Yes," said Sparkle. "I've found a

new home for the butterflies."

"Where? Will I still be able to visit them?" asked Isabel eagerly.

"Oh yes," said Sparkle, her eyes twinkling mischievously. "It's your garden."

"My garden?" Isabel was astounded. "But it's so small and there nothing in it."

"Butterflies don't need that much room," said Sparkle. "They need flowers. We can move the flowers growing here to your garden. They're going to be bulldozed when the builders start work. We'll move the plants whole, roots and all. So what do you think? Can the butterflies come and live with you?"

"It's a brilliant idea!" Isabel's face shone with excitement. "When can we start?"

"Now," said Sparkle.

She fluttered off Isabel's hand and flew to a clump of purple knapweed surrounded by butterflies. A pearly-white butterfly flew closer and tapped Sparkle on the wing. Sparkle shook her head.

"Sorry, but I can't play today. I've got a job to do."

Puzzled, the butterfly tapped Sparkle again then flew in the air, hovering above her.

Sparkle shook her head, hoping that when the butterfly saw her working she would understand. She was about to start her spell to dig up the knapweed when Isabel stopped her.

"How are you going to get the plants to my house?"

Sparkle wiggled her wings with embarrassment. She'd forgotten to ask Isabel if she'd carry them.

"We've got a wheelbarrow somewhere," said Isabel thoughtfully. "I think it's in the shed. I'll go home and look for it."

Isabel set off, her school bag bouncing on her back. Sparkle turned to the knapweed, clenching her wand while she worked out a spell to dig it up. Eventually she had one and, pointing the wand at the purple-headed plant, she chanted:

149

*"Dig up this plant, its leaves and shoots,
Purple flowers and all its roots."*

Immediately the wand grew warm and
the cluster of diamonds set in the gold star
sparkled and shone. The wand began to
hiss then a stream of red stars burst from it,
tumbling over the knapweed and making
it glitter. With a creaking noise the plant
started to move backwards and forwards.
The butterflies flew up in the air, their
colourful wings fluttering wildly. The plant
rocked faster and faster until, with a loud
ripping sound, its roots burst from the soil.

"Hooray," cheered Sparkle.

Next she pointed her wand at a
sprawling plant with large yellow daisy-
like flowers. It was hard work using magic
to dig up the flowers. Sparkle stopped for a
rest as Isabel returned, triumphantly pushing

a wheelbarrow with
a spade in it. The
butterflies that
had been hovering
overhead fluttered
away.

"Don't worry,"
said Sparkle
reassuringly. "They're
quite shy but they'll
come back when they
realize we're only *moving*
the plants."

"I hope you're right," said Isabel. "I
thought I'd help," she added, pointing at
the spade.

It took a long time to fill up the
wheelbarrow with plants, but at last Isabel
and Sparkle set off for Isabel's home.

"Luckily it's not too far," panted Isabel

as she pushed the wheelbarrow across the bumpy paving slabs.

Sparkle flew alongside her, calling out words of encouragement.

"I used to help Mum and Dad in the garden all the time at our old house," said Isabel, skilfully steering the barrow through

the side gate of her new home. She set it
down on the small patio. The flowerbed
was overgrown with weeds so Sparkle
used a little magic to help Isabel clear it.
Isabel squeaked with delight as the weeds
disappeared in a shower of red stars.

"Don't forget the stinging nettles," she
said, pointing to an untidy patch of green
plants.

Sparkle shook her head.

"Butterflies like to lay their eggs on
stinging nettles," she said.

Isabel looked at the plants with new
interest.

"I never knew stinging nettles were good
for butterflies. I've always hated them for
being ugly and because they sting. Mum's
right, then. She's always saying not to judge
things by the way they look."

Sparkle stared at Isabel, remembering

that Miss Alaska had said something similar to her last night.

Isabel set to work digging holes, filling them with water from the garden tap, placing the wild flowers in them and refilling the holes with soil. When Isabel had finished, the garden looked lovely but there was something missing. Butterflies! Hovering above the plants, Sparkle waved her wand:

*"Butterflies please come and settle
In your new home of flowers and nettles."*

Sparkle's wand hissed loudly and a flurry of red flower-scented stars cascaded over the plants. The stars sparkled and slowly dissolved in the afternoon sunshine. Then, as if holding its breath, the garden fell silent.

"What's that?" whispered Isabel, pointing

at a huge multicoloured cloud that seemed
to be moving closer. The cloud hung over
Isabel's garden for a moment and then
dramatically split apart.

"Hooray!" shouted Isabel, realizing
the cloud had been hundreds of brightly
coloured butterflies.

Sparkle somersaulted with delight.

"We did it!" she cried. "We gave the
butterflies a new home."

# Chapter Seven

More butterflies kept arriving until there wasn't a petal's space left to spare. Most of the newcomers hovered in the air, waiting for a turn on the flowers but a few pushy ones chased the smaller butterflies away.

"It's just like school," said Isabel crossly. "There's always at least one bully. We'll have to go back to the wasteland and dig up more flowers so there's room for everyone."

Sadly Sparkle shook her head.

"There aren't any flowers left to move –

only a flowering bush that was too big for your garden. I don't recognize all these butterflies. Maybe they've come from somewhere else."

Isabel fell silent, her hair flopping over her face and her eyes screwing up with concentration.

"I've got an idea," she said at last. "There's a big DIY store near here. I went there last weekend with Mum and Dad to get some stuff for the house. It sells garden plants too. I could use my pocket money to buy more plants. I've been saving for ages so I've got quite a bit. We could fill up the empty spaces in the flower bed, and the pots and window boxes at the front of the house."

Sparkle was amazed at Isabel's generosity. "Are you sure you don't mind spending your money on plants?" she asked.

"I'd love to," said Isabel excitedly. "It'll be much nicer living here with a butterfly garden. And the flowers might attract other wildlife as well."

Isabel ran inside to collect her purse then Sparkle rode on her shoulder to the DIY store. Isabel kept giggling.

"Your wings are tickling my neck," she complained.

"I can fly if it's annoying you," said Sparkle.

"No," said Isabel. "I like it."

Isabel was very different from the day Sparkle had seen her in the magic mirror. Her eyes danced with happiness, especially when she was choosing flowers for her new garden. Sparkle helped, pointing out the types she knew butterflies were particularly fond of. As Isabel pushed her trolley full of plants to the check out, she had a thought.

"How will I get this lot home?" she whispered to Sparkle, who was hiding in a plant.

"Are you all right? Did you lose your mum and dad?" asked the lady at the check out, hearing her whispering.

"Mum and Dad aren't here," said Isabel. "I'm doing up the garden as a surprise for them."

"What a lovely thing to do." The lady beamed at Isabel. "If you promise to bring the trolley back, then you can borrow it to take your plants home."

"I promise," said Isabel solemnly.

It was getting late by the time Isabel and Sparkle had planted the new flowers. The garden was transformed. It was bright, colourful and alive with butterflies.

"It reminds me of living in the country," sighed Isabel happily.

Sparkle was excited too. Not only had she completed her first task but she'd helped Isabel. She turned three somersaults, making her new friend laugh. The back door opened and Isabel's parents appeared, side by side with enormous grins on their faces.

"Isabel," said her mum, coming outside. "What a lovely surprise! You've planted flowers in the pots at the front of the house and just look at the back garden too. And you did it all on your own!"

"Well, sort of," said Isabel, hiding a grin as Sparkle dived behind a flower.

"Isabel, this is fantastic. I've been meaning to tidy the garden up since we moved. I was thinking there's room for a small pond if we dig up a corner of the grass," said Dad.

"A pond!" exclaimed Isabel. "Then we might get frogs."

"And dragonflies," said Dad. "Tell

you what. I'll just change out of my work clothes and we'll nip down to the DIY shop and see if they've got any pond stuff."

"Can we?" said Isabel. "Thanks, Dad. I'll return the trolley I borrowed at the same time."

"I'll come too," said Mum, enthusiastically. "I'll just go put some jeans on."

As the back door closed, Sparkle flew out of hiding.

"Are you coming with us?" asked Isabel. "Please say yes."

"I've got to go home," said Sparkle sadly. It would have been fun to watch Isabel and her parents choose the things they needed for a pond.

Isabel pulled a sad face.

"Will I see you again?"

"Yes," said Sparkle. She definitely

wanted to come back to visit Isabel and to check up on her wildlife garden. "It might not be for ages, but I will come back."

Isabel grinned. "I'm looking forward to it already! Thanks for everything, Sparkle. If it hadn't been for you, none of this would have happened."

Blushing, Sparkle fluttered her wings.

"We did it together," she said.

"Friends forever?" asked Isabel.

"Definitely," Sparkle replied. She swept her wand in the air and, closing her eyes, murmured the friendship spell she'd learned in Cub Class.

*"From me to you,*
*A star that's true."*

The wand almost jerked out of her paw as an enormous red star burst from it. Sparkle

164

caught the star between her
paws and handed it to
Isabel.

"A friendship star
to remember me
by," she said.

"Thank you!
It's beautiful,"
Isabel thanked
her.

Dad appeared at
the back door. "Isabel, are you ready?"

Isabel hid the star in her pocket.

"Bye, Sparkle. See you again one day."

"Bye, Isabel."

Sparkle flew in the air and was about to
fly home when an enormous butterfly with
orange-and-black wings flitted past. Sparkle
couldn't help but stare. That was the most
beautiful butterfly she'd ever seen. A smaller

butterfly thought so too and shyly squeaked a greeting. The large butterfly ignored the smaller one and, landing on a petal, vainly spread out her wings.

"Looks aren't everything," remembered Sparkle, dipping her wings at the smaller butterfly.

The little butterfly dipped his wings in a friendly salute back.

"It's what's on the inside that counts," finished Sparkle, smiling to herself as she headed home.

Fairy Bears Fact File

# Sparkle

1.  Favourite colour – *red*

    2.  Favourite gemstone – *ruby*

3.  Best flower – *rose*

    4.  Cutest animal – *foal*

5.  Birthday month – *June*

    6.  Yummiest food – *nectar*

7.  Favourite place – *the Butterfly Bridge*

    8.  Hobbies – *dancing*

9.  Best ever season – *summer*

    10.  Worst thing – *bedtime*

# A Puzzle for Primrose

# Chapter One

The class cave was empty when Primrose the Fairy Bear slipped inside. Primrose was always the first to arrive and she stood for a moment, her green wings quivering excitedly as she breathed in the familiar smell of the stone seats, tables and leaf note books. Primrose loved school! There was nothing better than putting her brain to work on the problems and puzzles that Miss Alaska set each day. Hurrying over to the teacher's desk she sorted through the pile of maths books until she found her own.

"Ten out of ten and a honey bee point!" sighed Primrose happily. Honey bee points were given as a reward for good work or good behaviour. Later Miss Alaska would give Primrose a bee-shaped token to put in her honey jar, and once the jar was full Primrose could exchange the tokens for a jar of real honey.

Primrose watched the door, impatiently waiting for Miss Alaska to arrive. What would they be doing today? Suddenly Primrose had a good idea. Maybe the magic mirror would give her a clue. She went and stood in front of it, staring into the rectangular-shaped glass. The tiny crystals decorating the frame sparkled brightly.

# A Puzzle for Primrose

"What are you trying to tell me?"
Primrose wondered aloud. But all she could
see was her own reflection: a happy bear
with striking gold fur and bright green
wings. Suddenly her reflection flickered and
then changed to show a cute white dog
curled up on a tartan rug. His nose rested
on his paws and there was a sad expression
on his whiskery face.

"Oh!" cried Primrose. "You poor thing.
Whatever can be wrong?"

The dog gave a deep sigh, but the mirror
was changing again. In a swirl of green
the little dog disappeared and the mirror
switched to a picture of a young girl sitting
in her bedroom colouring in a picture of
a basket of puppies. Primrose thought the
girl looked friendly. She had black hair
neatly plaited, which fell over one shoulder,
and the tip of her tongue stuck out of her

mouth as she concentrated. Primrose's eyes widened at the different shades of colouring pencils the girl was using, each one engraved with her name, Lucy.

"Hello, Lucy," whispered Primrose.

## A Puzzle for Primrose

She knew Lucy couldn't hear, but she watched her thoughtfully until the picture disappeared and her own reflection returned.

"What are you looking at?" asked Misty.

Primrose jumped. She'd been so engrossed by looking in the mirror that she hadn't noticed the classroom filling up.

"Hi, Misty, guess what!" she answered excitedly. "Today it's my turn to go out on a task. There's a girl called Lucy who needs my help. The mirror also showed me a picture of a sad little dog. I think the dog must belong to Lucy and she's too busy to play with him."

"Are you sure?" Misty sounded uncertain. "Miss Alaska normally gives out the tasks."

"Wait and see," said Primrose knowingly as Miss Alaska came into the classroom

175

carrying a large sycamore leaf.

"Good morning, class." Miss Alaska smiled at the Fairy Bears. "Dizzy, stop talking and listen, please. We have a busy day ahead. Written on this leaf is a task and the name of the Fairy Bear chosen to do it."

The Fairy Bears murmured excitedly. The tasks were very important – you had to pass all of them to be allowed to move up from the junior to the senior class. Miss Alaska was working her way through the

junior class, choosing one Fairy Bear at a time to take their first task. Primrose wriggled excitedly on her stool, certain that today it would be her turn!

"Before we start," said Miss Alaska, "let's say the Fairy Bear Promise."

Stone seats grated on the cave floor as the Fairy Bears stood up and held paws. Standing straight, with her green wings neatly folded behind her back, Primrose took hold of Misty's and Lulu's paws, closed her eyes and chanted along with the class.

"I promise to do my best. I promise to work hard to care for the world and all its plants, animals and children. This is the Fairy Bear Promise."

Primrose opened her eyes as Miss Alaska held up the sycamore leaf.

"This next task is for Primrose," she said, smiling straight at her.

"Thank you," replied Primrose as she took the leaf and read it quickly.

"Just what I thought," she said confidently. "My task is to help a West Highland Terrier called Sammy who's very sad and needs cheering up."

"Well done, clever paws," Misty teased her friend.

"That's not very exciting!" exclaimed Coral spitefully, wrinkling her nose. "I'm glad I didn't get that task."

"A task is as exciting as you want to make it," Primrose retorted.

She lifted her wand by its silver stem and gently rubbed the triangular-shaped jade gemstone set in its star. The green jewel sparkled brightly. Primrose waved the wand

and tiny green stars gushed out in a perfect arc.

"Well done, Primrose. That's wonderful wand work," said Miss Alaska. "Good luck, and remember to enjoy your task."

"I will," said Primrose, waving goodbye to Misty as she left the classroom.

There was a map on the sycamore leaf showing Primrose where to go once she'd left the Crystal Caves. It was a complicated journey but she was good at map reading. Primrose was also good at solving puzzles, and this one seemed easy. With a happy sigh Primrose began to rehearse what she would say to Lucy to convince her that Sammy was only sad because she was neglecting him.

# Chapter Two

The Main Tunnel was full of Fairy Bears queuing to get through the Grand Door. Primrose landed at the back of the line and tried not to get too frustrated at the hold up. She was in too much of a hurry to notice the beauty of the walls, studded with magically sparkling jewels, or the grandness of the gnarled root staircase at the end of the tunnel. Primrose hopped up the staircase and through the Grand Door, sighing happily as she arrived inside the hollow tree trunk that hid the Crystal Caves.

"At last!" said Primrose, her fur standing up with excitement.

Primrose blinked rapidly as her eyes adjusted to the dark. It was very quiet except for the hum of Fairy Bear wings all around her. Flapping her own wings quickly, Primrose flew upward and headed straight towards the pale circle of light shining above her. She knew it was coming from the forgotten squirrel hole, the way in and out of the sycamore tree. Primrose burst out into the daylight and sped across Firefly Meadow, not letting the lovely morning sunshine distract her.

She flew fast, enjoying the challenge of the journey. There were lots of changes in direction and each time she made a turn she hovered in the air carefully, checking the landmarks beneath her before she went on her way. A long while later Primrose

arrived at her
destination,
her furry
cheeks
flushed
with
excitement
from the
flight. The
house was a
small bungalow
with an overgrown
garden. Primrose
landed on a bush near
the gate and stared round
in surprise. This place looked far too small
and untidy to be Lucy and Sammy's home.
Hearing footsteps coming along the street
Primrose hurriedly pulled back until she was
completely hidden by leaves. The garden

gate groaned in protest as a man, dressed in a uniform and carrying a large bag, pushed it open and ran up the garden path.

"A postman," said Primrose in delight. She'd learned about them at school.

The postman was obviously in a hurry. He rammed a handful of letters into the letter box and jogged back down the garden path, leaving the gate swinging open behind him.

"Hello," called a friendly voice from the street. "Have you got any letters for us today?"

Suddenly the bush Primrose was resting on shook violently and a little white dog shot from underneath it and raced through the garden gate.

"Sammy!" exclaimed Primrose.

Gathering her wits together she flew after him.

# A Puzzle for Primrose

Sammy had a limp, but he was too determined to let that stop him. He ran across the road, hurling himself at a tall girl with long black hair, standing in her front garden clutching a handful of letters.

"Hello, Sammy!" The girl bent down and patted the dog, squealing with delight as he licked her hands and face.

"You're a bad dog," she gently scolded him. "You'll get run over crossing the road like that!"

Lucy? Primrose was so surprised she forgot

to be cautious and hovered in the air. The tall girl with the serious brown eyes was definitely the same girl she'd seen in the magic mirror. So Lucy wasn't Sammy's owner. She lived on the opposite side of the road in a large house with a pretty garden and two garages! Primrose had made a mistake by jumping to conclusions and was about to make another one . . . She was completely out in the open and, catching her scent in the air, Sammy quickly spun round.

"Woof, woof, woof," he barked in a friendly greeting.

"Sammy, shh! Mum's indoors trying to work . . ." Lucy stopped mid-sentence and took a step forward. Her mouth widened into an enormous smile. "Oh! You're so pretty. At first I thought you were a bumblebee, but you look more like a fairy close up."

## A Puzzle for Primrose

"I'm actually a Fairy Bear called Primrose."

Immediately Primrose knew she could trust Lucy, and she fluttered closer, hovering near the girl's pretty face.

"A Fairy Bear, that's so cute!" Lucy couldn't take her eyes off Primrose. "Are there lots of Fairy Bears?"

"Yes," said Primrose. "There are Fairy Bears all over the world."

"Even in the Arctic?" teased Lucy.

"Yes, and also Antarctica, North America, South America, Europe, Asia, Africa and Australasia." Primrose paused, trying to remember her continents.

"That's amazing," said Lucy. "So what exactly is a Fairy Bear?"

Primrose explained how Fairy Bears were related to the great bear Ursa Major and how once this great bear had helped a fairy with a damaged wing. Years later the same fairy had helped Ursa Major escape from hunters by turning him into a Fairy Bear. Lucy listened carefully.

"So Fairy Bears help animals, plants and children?" she asked when Primrose had finished explaining everything.

"That's right," said Primrose.

## A Puzzle for Primrose

"Who are you helping today, or is that a secret?" asked Lucy eagerly.

Primrose hesitated. Fairy Bears were very secretive, but all her Fairy Bear friends, who'd completed their first task, had met children and made friends with them. Sparkle had even brought a girl to the Crystal Caves for a visit. But, before she could answer, the front door opened and a tall lady with long dark hair like Lucy's stepped outside.

"There you are, Lucy. What are you doing out here?"

"Hi, Mum," said Lucy, sidestepping so that she was blocking Primrose from her mother's view. "Have you finished your work?"

"I've got a bit more to do, but I'm stopping for a tea break. Would you like a drink too?"

"Yes, please. I'll have a glass of orange juice," said Lucy. "But first I've got to take Sammy back across the road to Mrs Parker. He's escaped again!"

Lucy's mum laughed. "You and your animals! Don't be too long."

# Chapter Three

"Mum's an accountant," Lucy explained to Primrose as she carefully crossed the road. "She usually works in an office, but in the school holidays she's allowed to work at home. This week it's my half-term. Sometimes Mum lets me have a friend to play, but there aren't many children living around here so most of the time I'm on my own."

"That sounds lonely," said Primrose, who had lots of Fairy Bear friends living close by her home cave. In the holidays they had

great fun playing in each other's caves or
going out in a big group to visit the park
and all the different grottos.

"It can be lonely," said
Lucy. "I love animals and
I'd love a dog to keep me
company, but Mum and
Dad won't let me have one.
Mum says it wouldn't be
fair to leave a dog locked up
indoors when I'm at school
and she's at work."

"She's right," Primrose agreed,
remembering the lessons Miss Alaska had
given them on animal care. "It's much
better for dogs to have someone to keep
them company. They get bored when
they're left on their own and that's when
some dogs get into mischief."

Lucy giggled.

## A Puzzle for Primrose

"I know! My friend's dog Meg chews shoes when she's left alone."

"Sammy's limping," said Primrose anxiously as Lucy called the little dog to walk by her side.

"I noticed that too," said Lucy. "I haven't seen him out with Mrs Parker for days. Maybe that's why."

Primrose's brain was whirring. Her task had been to help Sammy. This must be why she was here, to cure his limp.

"Let me have a closer look," said Primrose. "Can you hold Sammy's collar and keep him still?"

"Of course," said Lucy. She crouched down and held the wriggling dog firmly by his tartan collar. "Good boy, Sammy."

193

Primrose fluttered down to the pavement and examined Sammy's leg. His white fur was so matted it was hard to see anything. Carefully, she used the tip of her wand to push the fur aside. The closer she got to Sammy's paw the more he began to squirm.

"Steady, boy," said Lucy soothingly. "Primrose is going to help you."

There was nothing wrong with the top of the paw but it was too big and heavy for Primrose to lift it up to look at the paw pad. Taking a deep breath Primrose waved her wand at Sammy's leg.

> *"Little Sammy, lift your paw,*
> *Show me why it looks so sore."*

As the spell ended, glittering green stars burst from Primrose's wand and fell on Sammy. The little dog sneezed and then his

eyes widened in surprise as his paw began
to rise in the air.

"That's amazing," Lucy gasped. "Can
you do lots of magic?"

But Primrose didn't hear. She was too
absorbed in the task of finding out what
was wrong with Sammy's leg.

"Look at that!" she exclaimed. "Poor
Sammy has a huge thorn stuck in his paw.

Lucy's plait fell over her shoulder as she bent forward to look. She pushed it away.

"Ooh! That's nasty. Sammy needs to see the vet."

"No he doesn't." Puffing out her golden chest Primrose fluttered her wings importantly. "I can sort this out."

"Is that your task?" asked Lucy.

"Yes," said Primrose, her mind racing through all the spells she knew. Removing a thorn from an animal was quite advanced magic. Primrose was flattered that Miss Alaska had chosen her for such a difficult task and determined to get it right first time. She took a slow deep breath to calm herself then, lifting her wand and pointing it at the thorn, she recited the spell.

*"Nasty big thorn in Sammy's paw,*
*Fall out now and land on the floor."*

196

## A Puzzle for Primrose

The silver handle of Primrose's wand
began to tremble. Primrose gripped it and
held it tightly, even though the vibrations
grew so strong they made her paw shake.
There was a whooshing noise followed
by a jet of green stars that rushed out of
the wand's tip and fell in a glittering haze
around Sammy's paw. For a few seconds
Sammy's leg sparkled green. Then, as the
stars evaporated, the thorn magically began
to wriggle free. Eventually it fell from
Sammy's paw and on to
the pavement, leaving
behind a nasty wound.
Panting slightly
Primrose rested
on Lucy's hand.

"Are you
OK?" asked
Lucy.

"Yes, thanks, but that was strong magic. It makes you feel out of breath, like when you've been in a flying race."

Primrose pulled herself together and pointed her wand at Sammy's paw and chanted:

*"As Sammy licks,*
*Let the wound fix."*

Green stars rushed from Primrose's wand, forming a glimmering circle around Sammy's whiskery muzzle. In a daze Sammy lowered his head, stuck out his pink tongue and carefully licked his paw. With each lick the wound began to heal until there was no trace of an injury.

"Wow!" breathed Lucy. "Primrose, you are so clever."

"It was nothing," said Primrose modestly,

her brown
eyes shining
with pride.

Suddenly
Sammy
lay flat on
the ground
then,
stretching out his head, he gently nudged
Primrose with the tip of his black nose.

"That's so sweet. He's saying thank
you," declared Lucy.

"I haven't finished yet," said Primrose,
lifting her wand again.

> *"Groom Sammy until he's fluffy,*
> *Make his coat as soft as a puppy."*

The wand shuddered then fell still. Primrose
screwed up her eyes in concentration and

chanted the words again, but still nothing happened. She almost stamped her paw with frustration.

"It's because I'm tired," she said. "I need to rest before I can do any more spells."

An excited look crossed Lucy's face.

"We don't need magic," she gabbled. "We can comb Sammy's fur with one of my doll's brushes. Wait in my front garden and I'll go and get one."

Lucy rushed indoors and a short while later came back with a small brush. Gently she combed out Sammy's knotted fur while Primrose picked out pieces of twigs and grass seeds.

"That was great fun and he looks lovely," said Lucy, standing back to admire their work. "Come on, boy. It's time to go home."

"It's time for me to go too," said

# A Puzzle for Primrose

Primrose. She felt sad having to say
goodbye to Lucy so soon after meeting her,
but she was also fizzing with happiness.
She'd done it! She'd passed her first task. It
had been much easier than she'd imagined.
All her other friends had taken two days
to complete their first tasks but she'd done

hers in one. Resisting the urge to fly a somersault, in case Lucy thought she was showing off, Primrose fluttered into the air and hovered in front of Lucy.

"Do you have to go straight away?" asked Lucy. "We've only just met."

Primrose hesitated. It would be fun to play with Lucy, but what if Miss Alaska awarded her with extra marks for quickness?

"Sorry, I have to go straight home. But we can play another day."

"Really? I'd love that!" Lucy's eyes sparkled. "See you soon, Primrose."

"See you soon," said Primrose, waving her wand at Lucy as she soared into the air.

Primrose had an excellent memory. She didn't need to check the map on her sycamore leaf to find the way home. She flew fast, skilfully avoiding the winged insects flying around her, and was back at the Crystal Caves in time for lunch.

# Chapter Four

Primrose hurried across the playground, her nose twitching in delight at the delicious smells coming from the dining cave. The rest of her class were already sitting at a long stone table and tucking into their meals. Primrose waved to Misty, grinning happily at the surprised look on her friend's face.

I bet she didn't expect me back so soon, thought Primrose smugly as the dinner-lady bear handed her a generous portion of honeycomb and a bowl of fruit salad. She helped herself to a glass of nectar from the drinks bar and then joined her friends.

"Squeeze up."

"It's all right, I'm not stopping. I'm going to play air ball," said Lulu, gulping down the rest of her nectar and standing up.

"Thanks, Lulu," said Primrose, sitting down next to Misty.

"Lulu is sport mad!" exclaimed Misty, her blue wings fluttering impatiently. "She didn't remember to ask you how you got on."

"Never mind," said Primrose cheerfully. "It was much easier than I thought. Sammy had a thorn in his paw so I took it out and did a healing spell, then a really nice girl called Lucy—"

"You did a healing spell!" shrieked Misty. "They're really difficult, Primrose!"

## A Puzzle for Primrose

Primrose went pink with pleasure.

"I know," she said, proudly wiggling her wings.

Lunchtime passed very quickly for Primrose, who kept being asked to tell how she'd solved her first task.

"Lucy sounds really nice," said Misty wistfully. "What a shame you didn't have longer with her."

"I said I'd go and visit her again," said Primrose.

The end-of-lunch bell sounded and Primrose leaped up, eager to return to class and tell Miss Alaska her exciting news. Miss Alaska's yellow-and-pink wings fluttered in surprise when Primrose entered the class cave.

"Hello, Primrose. I didn't expect you back so soon."

Primrose blushed prettily.

"I've finished my task," she said, handing Miss Alaska the sycamore leaf that her teacher had given her earlier.

"I don't think you have," said Miss Alaska, folding her paws together and refusing to take the leaf.

Primrose wiggled the leaf at Miss Alaska.

"I have. Sammy had a thorn stuck in his

paw. I took it out and healed the wound."

"Your task was to cheer Sammy up," Miss Alaska pointed out.

"He is cheerful now the thorn's gone," insisted Primrose.

"Let me show you something," said Miss Alaska. She led Primrose to the magic mirror and made her stand in front of it.

"What do you see?"

Primrose stared at her reflection, waiting for it to disappear and show her a picture of Sammy looking happy. A swirling grey mist seeped across the mirror, clouding the glass and blotting out Primrose's image. Suddenly the mist cleared and there was Sammy curled up in his basket, with his nose on his paws, still looking very sad. Primrose was dumbstruck. Whatever was wrong with the little dog now? She stared at the picture, hoping to work it out, but

the picture was fading already and a new one forming. Here was Lucy, sprawled on a massive bean bag, totally engrossed in a book. Primrose frowned. There had to be a connection between Sammy's unhappiness and Lucy, but for the life of her Primrose couldn't see what.

An unpleasant laugh snapped Primrose out of her thoughts.

"Ha!" said Coral scornfully. "Little Miss Clever Paws is stuck for a change. How does it feel, Primrose, knowing you've failed your task?"

210

## A Puzzle for Primrose

"Primrose hasn't failed her task. She just hasn't completed it yet," said Miss Alaska sharply. "Sometimes things aren't as obvious as they seem. You have to look deeper to find out what the true problem is."

Primrose shot Miss Alaska a grateful look. She wasn't sure what her teacher meant by looking deeper, but she was determined to try to solve the puzzle by herself.

"I'll go straight back," she said, walking to the door.

"Not today," said Miss Alaska gently. "Take the afternoon off school and go and think about what you've been asked to do."

Take the afternoon off school! Primrose opened her mouth to protest, but catching the look on Miss Alaska's face shut it again quickly. Wings drooping dejectedly she

picked up her wand
and shuffled out of
the class cave. Where
should she go? She
needed peace and
quiet to think and she
wouldn't get any at
her home cave with
her little brothers there,
who were twins and very noisy.

Not knowing where to go Primrose
wandered along the Main Tunnel, heading
in the opposite direction to the Grand Door
until she passed the play park. A tiny Fairy
Bear clutching a toy wand was playing
on the roundabout while his mum sat on
a bench reading. The swings, Primrose's
favourite park equipment, were empty.
Without thinking Primrose unlatched the
jewel-studded gate shaped like a castle door

and went into the park, sitting down on a
swing. The swaying movement was very
soothing. Primrose rocked back and forth
idly watching the little bear playing. Faster
and faster he spun the roundabout and then
he leaped on, squealing with delight as he
whizzed round and round.

*"Sometimes things aren't as obvious as they seem. You have to look deeper to find out what the true problem is."*

Miss Alaska's words echoed in Primrose's head but what did her teacher mean? Primrose had to work it out to help poor Sammy. If she didn't, Sammy would stay sad and she'd fail her first task. It was a shocking thought to clever Primrose.

"Maybe I'm not so clever," she wondered aloud.

The little Fairy Bear on the roundabout was bouncing up and down.

"Faster," he shouted, waving a paw and accidentally letting go of his wand. The toy wand flew through the air, bounced on the ground and slid under the roundabout. The Fairy Bear slowed the roundabout with his paw then jumped off. He lay on his tummy and tried to reach the wand, but his arms weren't long enough and he burst into tears.

On the stone bench his mother jumped up in alarm.

"Rufus!" she cried, rushing over. "What happened?"

The mother gathered the howling Fairy Bear into her arms, patting his back as she searched for an injury. Primrose jumped off her swing and rushed over.

# Chapter Five

Primrose tried to get the mother's attention to tell her what had happened. "He's not hurt – he's lost his wand."

But she didn't seem to hear her, so Primrose pointed her wand at the bottom of the roundabout and chanted.

*"Toy wand, come to me,*
*At the count of one, two, THREE!"*

Warmth rushed through the silver stem of Primrose's wand. The triangular jade jewel sparkled then three green stars whizzed out and disappeared under the roundabout. There was a funny squeaking noise and suddenly the toy wand slid out from where it'd been lost and came to rest at Primrose's paws. She picked it up and handed it to Rufus, who immediately stopped crying.

"Oh, Rufus! You gave me such a fright. I thought you'd hurt yourself," said the mother Fairy Bear with relief.

"Thank you," said Rufus, beaming at Primrose.

"Yes, thank you," his mum added.

"You're welcome," said Primrose, glad that she'd made someone happy. Thoughtfully she walked back to the swings. That mother had wrongly thought Rufus had injured himself playing, whereas Primrose had been able to help because she'd seen what had happened. Suddenly Miss Alaska's words began to make sense. Primrose had to find out more about Sammy to discover what was making him unhappy. Primrose was sure the magic mirror was giving her a clue by showing her Lucy at the same time as Sammy. But how were they linked? Primrose couldn't work it out. Feeling frustrated she hurried home. If only it was morning already so that she could restart her task and find a way to help Sammy!

★

# A Puzzle for Primrose

Primrose woke early and ate a hurried breakfast of honey-soaked toast and nectar juice. She hugged her parents, waved at her brothers (who were too sticky to hug) and set out for the Grand Door. There was hardly anyone else about as it was too early for most Fairy Bears to start work. Primrose flew along the Main Tunnel to the huge Grand Door, which was still closed. On nimble paws she hopped up the gnarled root staircase and reached up for the sycamore-leaf-shaped handle. It was exciting opening the door by herself.

Primrose traced her paw over the wooden handle, feeling the engravings that made it look like

219

a real leaf. Her fur was tingling with anticipation as she pulled open the door, sighing happily as the darkness rushed out to meet her. Bouncing lightly on her paws Primrose leaped into the air and flew up the dark tree trunk until a small circle of light shining through the squirrel hole beckoned her closer. Without stopping Primrose darted through the squirrel hole and turned a joyful somersault as she arrived outside.

It was a glorious morning. The sun spread out across a pale blue sky, spilling light on the colourful flowers scattered across Firefly Meadow. Primrose took a deep breath, inhaling the fresh morning air and the perfume of the flowers. She was determined to take things more slowly today, and find out exactly what was wrong with Sammy. At last she set off on her journey, her green wings beating so fast she could have been mistaken for a dragonfly zipping through the air.

It was still early morning when she flew over Sammy's bungalow. Dipping down Primrose was just in time to see the front door open a crack.

"Out you go," said an elderly voice.

Sammy's whiskery face squeezed through the door, his nose twitching as he sampled the morning air.

"Hurry up!" said Mrs Parker, with a note of impatience this time.

Casually Sammy walked into the front garden and began to sniff under the bushes.

For a moment Primrose was cross. Lazy Mrs Parker! Why didn't she take Sammy for a walk instead of just putting him out in the garden? Dogs loved going on walks and there was a park nearby. Primrose had just flown over it. Suddenly, remembering Rufus and the lost wand, Primrose checked her thoughts. She mustn't jump to conclusions. There might be a good reason for Mrs Parker's behaviour and it was up to Primrose to find out the facts. She would go and see Lucy first. Maybe she could help.

Leaving Sammy snuffling in the bushes, Primrose soared quickly across the road to Lucy's house. The front door was closed so Primrose flew around the house, peering in the windows. There was no sign of Lucy downstairs, only her mum, typing away at a computer in a room with a huge desk and lots of bookcases. Starting at the front

# A Puzzle for Primrose

of the house Primrose flew up to the first-floor windows. She found Lucy straight away, lying on her tummy in the middle of her bedroom, reading a book about dogs. The window was open so Primrose went inside and landed on a picture of a dog that looked like Sammy.

"Primrose!" Lucy was surprised and delighted to see her. "Have you come to play with me?"

"Not today," said Primrose honestly. "I've come back because I haven't finished my task and I hoped you might be able to help me."

"Me?" Lucy's brown eyes shone. "I'd love to. What do you want me to do?"

Primrose explained about Sammy and how she thought she'd solved the problem of his unhappiness but hadn't. When she'd finished, Lucy got up and stood beside the window looking out on to the street.

"I used to see Mrs Parker out with Sammy every day," she said thoughtfully. "But lately she hardly goes out at all. She wasn't very friendly when I took Sammy back yesterday. Usually she talks for ages. She loves hearing about school and all the things I've been doing, but yesterday she was acting strangely. She opened the door just enough to see who it was then made poor Sammy squeeze inside. Maybe she doesn't want him any more. It's not fair! I'd love to have a dog."

Surely Mrs Parker hadn't grown tired of Sammy? Primrose didn't want to believe that. There had to be another reason. She fluttered over to the window and landed on Lucy's hand.

"Look," said Lucy suddenly. "What's Sammy doing? He's got his head under the fence."

"He must have dug a hole," said Primrose. "Quick, Lucy! He's escaping again."

Primrose darted through the open window and into the street while Lucy ran downstairs. Sammy's head and shoulders were already through the hole and he wriggled like a stuck snake as he tried to get the rest of his body through. Across the street Lucy's front door opened and she heard Lucy call out to her mum, "Sammy's escaped again. Can I go after him?"

Primrose didn't hear the reply because at that moment Sammy gave a satisfied grunt and, wriggling free, he set off down the road. His tail was just disappearing round the corner as Lucy came outside and carefully crossed over to Mrs Parker's house.

"He went that way," said Primrose, pointing.

"Let's go," said Lucy, setting off at a fast jog.

## A Puzzle for Primrose

She ran down the road, while Primrose flew alongside her. Reaching the corner they saw Sammy at the end of the next road.

"Sammy!" called Lucy, but the little dog kept going, his tail wagging cheerfully as he galumphed along.

"He's heading towards the park where Mrs Parker used to walk him," panted Lucy at the end of the next street. She ran  fast and Primrose frantically beat her wings to keep up. Soon they reached the park and Lucy stepped through the iron gates shouting, "Sammy, here, boy!"

The park was full of children playing, and dogs on leads sedately walking alongside their owners, but there was no sign of Sammy anywhere.

# Chapter Six

Primrose wasn't happy about flying low over such a crowded place.

"Can I ride on your shoulder so your hair hides me?" she asked Lucy.

"I'd love that!" Lucy replied excitedly.

Primrose flew down and hid behind Lucy's long black hair, using her wand to part the hair enough for her to peek out. Lucy jogged round the park calling Sammy's name. About halfway round she stopped suddenly and reached down, pulling a tartan collar with a round metal disc attached out of a flower bed.

"Oh no!" she gasped. "It's Sammy's collar. It must have fallen off. We've got to find him quickly. Mrs Parker's address is on this tag. If Sammy gets lost, then no one will know where he lives so they won't be able to take him home."

"It looks like he went that way," Primrose said, pointing at the trampled flowers.

## A Puzzle for Primrose

"Yes, it does," Lucy agreed.

She picked her way through the flower bed, being careful not to cause any more damage as she followed Sammy's paw prints.

"Look!" Lucy gasped at the overturned litter bin lying across the path. "I bet Sammy did that too."

She went to pick it up but Primrose stopped her.

"Let me," she said.

Checking there was no one around Primrose pointed her wand at the bin and chanted.

*"Stand up, bin,*
*Litter back in."*

Warmth flooded through her wand as a river of stars burst from the end. The

231

bin began to rock, faster and faster until suddenly it tipped itself the right way up and set itself back on the path. The scattered rubbish magically came to life and danced up in the air, before jumping inside the bin.

"Cool!" breathed Lucy. "If only we could use your magic to find Sammy."

"Sorry, but it's not strong enough to do that," said Primrose, her wings drooping.

"Don't be sorry. There are lots of things I haven't learned to do yet. Your magic is brilliant," said Lucy kindly.

"Do you think so?"

"Yes," said Lucy firmly.

They searched the rest of the park, hurriedly putting to right any damage Sammy had caused. There was a knocked over bicycle, two more overturned dustbins and lots of trampled flowers.

"He's not here," sighed Lucy, her eyes bright with unshed tears.

"He can't have gone far," said Primrose, sounding more positive than she felt. "Let's look one more time."

Suddenly Primrose's ears began to twitch. What was that sound? She listened carefully until she heard it again.

"Woof, woof, woof."

"Sammy," shouted Lucy and Primrose together.

"It's coming from the duck pond," said Primrose.

233

Lucy wheeled round and gasped as she noticed the duck house on the island in the middle of the pond.

"Oh, Sammy, now what have you done?"

"He's stuck!" Primrose started to giggle and so did Lucy and soon neither of them could stop. Naughty Sammy had the ducks' metal water bowl wedged on his head, making him too big to get out of the duck house.

"Now what?" said Lucy, hiccupping with laughter. "Do you think the water's shallow enough for me to wade over and rescue him?"

"You'd better ask a grown-up to help you," said Primrose sensibly. "What about that man over there wearing a uniform?"

"That's the park warden," said Lucy. "Hide under my hair, Primrose, and I'll go and ask him for help."

Luckily the park warden was very nice
and didn't get cross when Lucy explained
how Sammy was stuck in the duck house.
He fetched a pair of waders from his hut
and put them on, ready to rescue Sammy.

"Eeek," laughed the warden, handing
the soggy dog over to Lucy. "I'm wetter
from being licked than I am from being in
the pond."

"Thank you," said Lucy gratefully. With
nimble fingers she fastened Sammy's collar
back round his neck. The park warden lent
her a dog lead he kept in his hut, especially
for lost dogs, and Lucy thanked him again.

"Take care walking him home," joked
the warden. "He's a tiny terror that one.
He's probably bored. You ought to take
him out more."

"Sammy's not mine. But I'll tell his

owner. And thanks for the loan of the dog
lead," she added.

Once they had left the park Primrose
came out of hiding and flew alongside
Lucy. Sammy seemed very happy,
bouncing along at the end of the lead, and
Lucy was ecstatic.

"This is the first time I've ever walked a
dog," she smiled. "If I had my own dog, I'd
take him for walks every day, even in the
rain!"

They turned the corner into the end of
Lucy's road and Primrose noticed that both
Lucy and Sammy seemed to slow down as
if neither of them wanted the walk to be
over. By the time they reached Mrs Parker's
gate they were crawling along like two
snails. Primrose fluttered down and hid on
Lucy's shoulder again when she knocked
on Mrs Parker's door. Mrs Parker took ages

to answer. Primrose was glad. It gave her extra time to think about her task. She'd rescued Sammy twice now, but she still hadn't found out why the little dog was unhappy. Primrose gave a big sigh. All her friends had completed their tasks in two days. This was Primrose's second day and

she was still no closer to solving the puzzle. Would Miss Alaska give her extra time? It would be embarrassing to take longer than everyone else to complete her first task, but it would be much better than failing it. Failing would mean spending an extra year in the juniors. Primrose's green wings went ice cold at the thought.

# Chapter Seven

Once again Mrs Parker didn't open the front door fully and made poor Sammy squeeze inside.

"Thank you," she said shortly, then closed the door with a bang.

"Well!" Lucy was outraged. "What's wrong with her? She used to be so nice."

Primrose came out of hiding and hovered near Lucy's face.

"Mrs Parker's got a secret. Did you notice the way her eyes kept wandering to something hidden behind the door?"

## A Puzzle for Primrose

"Oh! I just thought she wasn't being very friendly," said Lucy. "I wonder what she's got to hide."

"I'll take a look," Primrose offered.

Primrose flew round the bungalow peeping in all the windows until she'd circled the whole house. Lucy was sitting on the doorstep waiting for her to return.

"Well?" she asked, jumping up.

Primrose shook her head. "All the curtains were drawn so I couldn't see a thing. But there is another way."

Primrose pointed her wand at the letter box.

*"Letter box, letter box, open wide,*
*And let this Fairy Bear fly inside."*

In a flash of green a flurry of stars cascaded
from Primrose's wand and landed on the
letter box. Primrose held her breath. Had
the spell been strong enough to work? Very
slowly the letter box began to open until
it was wide enough for Primrose to fly
through. Then the flap stopped moving and
held itself out, so it looked like a tongue
poking from the letter box's
metal mouth.

# A Puzzle for Primrose

"Wow! Primrose you're so clever," whispered Lucy.

Primrose blushed. Being clever didn't feel as important as it used to. It was how you used your knowledge that counted.

"I won't be long," she whispered back, taking a deep breath and trying to steady her nerves as she flew inside Mrs Parker's house.

The drawn curtains made it very dark inside but Primrose liked that. Mrs Parker's house felt small and cluttered compared to Lucy's. Every surface was covered with photographs of Sammy and ornaments of dogs. Mrs Parker was obviously keen on dogs so what was going on? There were only four rooms and a tiny bathroom so it didn't take long for Primrose to explore. Knowing Mrs Parker was in the kitchen Primrose investigated that room last. Her heart thumped nervously and her wings trembled as she flew inside, keeping close to the ceiling where she wouldn't be spotted.

Mrs Parker was leaning on the kitchen worktop, waiting for a kettle to boil. Her gnarled hands gripped the counter tightly and her face was creased with pain. Leaning against her was a walking stick. Sammy lay on a tartan blanket, eyes closed and grunting contentedly after his adventure in the park.

Primrose flew nearer. There was a crude bandage round Mrs Parker's leg that didn't look like it had been put on by a doctor or nurse. The kettle boiled and switched itself off with a loud click that made Primrose jump.

It took Mrs Parker ages to make herself a drink. She had to put the kettle down three times to steady herself. Using the stick for support she shuffled out of the kitchen,

the drink wobbling in the cup as she slowly
made her way to her lounge.

Primrose had seen enough. Quickly she
flew back through the letter box, which
closed behind her. Lucy was still waiting on
the step.

"You were a long time," she said
anxiously.

"Mrs Parker's hurt her leg," said
Primrose. "She's using a stick and she can
hardly walk."

"So that's why she hasn't been taking
Sammy out!" Lucy exclaimed.

"Hmm," mused Primrose as an idea
began to shape in
her mind. "Lucy,
why don't you
offer to walk
Sammy for Mrs
Parker? Then

she wouldn't have to leave him out in the garden where he gets bored and lonely."

"That's a brilliant idea. I'd have to ask Mum first, but I'm sure she'd say yes. It'll be like having my own dog!" said Lucy happily. "I'll go and ask her right now!"

Lucy's mum thought it was a great idea too.

"Tell Mrs Parker that if she needs anything from the shops I'll get it for her. I'll also drive her to the doctor's if she wants to see one," she added.

"Thanks, Mum."

Lucy's eyes sparkled merrily as she went back to their neighbour's house with Primrose flying beside her. Primrose hid in a bush when Lucy knocked on the door. She waited impatiently even though she knew it would take Mrs Parker ages to answer with her hurt leg. At last there came the sound of shuffling and the front door opened a crack.

"Hello, Lucy, what is it this time?" said Mrs Parker irritably.

Lucy flushed and suddenly became tongue tied. Primrose hoped she'd remember that Mrs Parker was grumpy because she was in pain.

"I was wondering if you'd like any help walking and grooming Sammy?" said Lucy in a rush. "It's the half-term holiday so I've got lots of free time."

Mrs Parker stared at Lucy for a moment then her wrinkled face broke into a huge smile.

"That would be marvellous," she said. "I've hurt my leg, you see, and I can't get out. Poor Sammy's rather sad. He does love his walks."

"Mum says she'll get your shopping and take you to the doctor's."

Primrose groaned. How was Lucy going to explain that she knew about Mrs Parker's leg? But she needn't have worried. Mrs Parker burst out laughing until she had to reach for her walking stick hidden behind the door to steady herself.

## A Puzzle for Primrose

"I thought I'd managed to keep that a secret," she chortled. "I was worried that if anyone found out I couldn't take Sammy for walks they'd think it was cruel and take him away from me. I didn't want that to happen. Sammy's all I've got."

"Poor you," said Lucy sympathetically. "But you can always ask me when you need help. I love dogs, especially cute ones like Sammy."

"Thank you, Lucy. You can borrow Sammy any time you like. He's always happy to go on a walk."

Lucy arranged to take Sammy for another walk to the park that afternoon so she could return the borrowed dog lead. Mrs Parker looked much happier as she said goodbye.

"It's time for me to go," said Primrose, once they were back in Lucy's garden.

"I'm going to really miss you," sighed Lucy. "But at least I've got Sammy to keep me company. I can't wait to walk him this afternoon. I'm going to ask Mrs Parker if I can borrow his brush and groom him afterwards."

"He'll love that," said Primrose. Then she added, "I'm going to miss you too. Thank you for helping me with my task."

Primrose's stomach fizzed with excitement. She'd done it. She'd finally discovered what Sammy's problem was and by fixing it she'd completed her first task. With Lucy's help, of course! The task had made Primrose realize that everyone needs help sometimes. Fluttering into the air Primrose hovered in front of Lucy's face.

"There's one last thing before I go."

With a grand sweep of her wand

## A Puzzle for Primrose

Primrose recited a friendship spell she'd
learned back in Cub Class.

> *"From me to you,*
> *A star that's true!"*

Primrose's wand began to tremble until
suddenly with a loud
crack a bright green
star popped out of
the end. Catching
it in both paws she
offered it to Lucy.

"A friendship
star," she said
simply.

"Thank you!"
Lucy's eyes were
as round as dinner plates as she
carefully took the star from Primrose.

"I'll keep it in my jewellery box and look at it every day."

"Bye, Lucy." Primrose fluttered higher.

"Bye!" Lucy waved back, smiling.

Primrose could feel Lucy's eyes watching her as she rose into the air. She wasn't usually impulsive and she didn't want to show off but she couldn't help herself. With

an extra beat of her wings she turned three somersaults and two cartwheels. Hearing Lucy chuckle Primrose giggled too.

Primrose couldn't wait to tell Miss Alaska how by learning not to jump to conclusions she'd completed her task. Dipping her wings in a final goodbye, Primrose flew home to the Crystal Caves.

# Primrose

1. Favourite colour – *green*

    2. Favourite gemstone – *peridot*

3. Best flower – *primrose*

    4. Cutest animal – *rabbit*

5. Birthday month – *April*

    6. Yummiest food – *honeycomb*

7. Favourite place – *School Caves*

    8. Hobbies – *solving puzzles*

9. Best ever season – *spring*

    10. Worst thing – *laziness*

# Time for Some . . .

# Fairy Bear Puzzle Fun!

# Blossom's Quiz

I love living in the Crystal Caves, and performing magic is fun! Chose the right word from the list below to answer the Fairy Bear questions.

| | | |
|---|---|---|
| fly | Promise | honey |
| tasks | wand | Firefly |

1)    The Crystal Caves are hidden underneath a sycamore tree in _ _ _ _ _ _ _ Meadow.

2)    Fairy Bears are about the size of a bumble bee and can _ _ _.

3)    Fairy Bears perform spells by using a magic _ _ _ _.

4)    In the Nectar Cave, we trade nectar for _ _ _ _ _ with the bees.

5)    We chant the Fairy Bear _ _ _ _ _ _ _ every day in school.

6)    Fairy Bears must perform special _ _ _ _ _ so that they can move up to the next class.

# Sparkle's Wordsnake

Helping the butterflies was hard work but it felt so great to find them a new home and pass my task! See if you can find all the words below hidden in my winding wordsnake. The words go in one continuous line, up and down, backwards and forwards, but never diagonally.

```
S  P  A  S  E
L  K  R  I  M
E  D  I  R  O
O  M  A  P  S
N  S  T  A  R
D  N  E  D  R
B  U  T  G  A
R  E  T  K  S
F  L  Y  T  A
```

SPARKLE    DIAMOND    BUTTERFLY
TASK    GARDEN    STARS    PROMISE

# Your Fact File

- - - - - - -

1. Favourite colour _ _ _ _ _ _ _
2. Favourite gemstone _ _ _ _ _ _ _
3. Best flower _ _ _ _ _ _ _
4. Cutest animal _ _ _ _ _ _ _
5. Birthday month _ _ _ _ _ _ _
6. Yummiest food _ _ _ _ _ _ _
7. Favourite place _ _ _ _ _ _ _
8. Hobbies _ _ _ _ _ _ _
9. Best ever season _ _ _ _ _ _ _
10. Worst thing _ _ _ _ _ _ _

# Tales from the Crystal Caves

## Julie Sykes

Fairy Bears work hard, helping to care for the world – and they love to make new friends! Can **Misty** save a baby owl? Will **Lulu** help a little girl to pass her skipping challenge? And how can **Poppy** make a birthday wish come true?

**Three more sparkly stories in one book!**